THE THIRTEENTH MEMBER

THE THIRTEENTH MEMBER

Mollie Hunter

CANONGATE · KELPIES

First published 1971 by Hamish Hamilton, London
First published in Kelpies 1986

copyright © Mollie Hunter 1971

Cover illustration by Jill Downie

Printed in Great Britain
by Cox & Wyman Ltd, Reading, Berkshire

ISBN 0 86241 112 2

*The publisher acknowledges subsidy
of the Scottish Arts Council
towards the publication of this volume.*

CANONGATE PUBLISHING LTD
17 JEFFREY STREET, EDINBURGH EH1 1DR

Contents

Chapter 1

INCIDENT AT NIGHT

The light travelling slowly seawards was blueish in colour. It moved unevenly, bobbing and jerking just above hedgerow level, and its pale glow was eerie in the summer darkness.

It was neither torch nor lantern, Adam Lawrie decided. Its glow was too wide-spread for either of those, and its colour was more like that of a—of a corpse-candle! He shivered at the thought, wishing he could dismiss it in sleep again, and reached clumsily for his one ragged blanket.

It was hunger that had first roused him to a sight of the light's ghostly dancing, the never-satisfied hunger of sixteen years growing rapidly to man's height. Now cold was helping to keep him awake, for the outhouse in Master Seton's stable-yard was a draughty place at the best of times, and that July of 1590 had not escaped the chill wind which blows so often on Scotland's east coast. Adam clutched his blanket close against it, and went resentfully back to his watch at the window-slit of the outhouse.

Below him in the darkness, the long sweep of Birsley Brae dropped down from his own village of Tranent to that of Prestonpans on the sea coast. The light, he noted, was following the line of the track winding between the two places, which meant he could rule out the possibility of a will-o'-the-wisp dancing random over the fields. Yet what else could it be? Adam pondered the question, feeling strongly tempted to slip out for a closer look that might provide the answer to it.

And why not? he asked himself. It was no part of common-sense, of course, to pursue strange lights at night, and he would surely be whipped if Master Seton discovered him abroad at this late hour. But surely also, it was worth while taking any risk that would distract his mind from these gnaw-

ing hunger-pains. And besides, it was most unlikely that anyone else would be awake to spy on his night-prowling and
report it to Master Seton.

Reassured by this last thought Adam cast off his blanket,
and was immediately confounded by a glimpse of a figure
moving stealthily across the stable-yard.

It was a girl's figure—a small and slender girl who
clutched cautiously at the skirts of her gown as she glided
past the outhouse. The shawl she wore was pulled well forward to hide her face, but there was no-one else of that slight
build in the Seton household, and Adam's shock of dismay
vanished as he recognised her. Silently, with a kind of amused
scorn, he shaped her name.

Gilly Duncan! Timid little kitchenmaid Gilly to be out
alone at such an hour! In all the three months she had been
in Seton's employ, Adam thought, he had never known her do
anything so daring; and yielding to an impulse that pushed
his original intention to the back of his mind, he went quickly
out into the stable-yard.

Gilly was making for the gate that led out to the path skirting the paddock, and soundless on his bare feet he padded
after her. As she reached the path's end, however, the obvious
reason for her actions occurred to him, and he hung back
feeling suddenly ashamed of his curiosity.

Beyond the path lay a meadow with the rounded tower of
Master Seton's newly-built dove-cote looming high at its
centre, and gossip said that the village courting-couples were
already fixing on this as their meeting-place. Adam hesitated,
peering across the meadow, but went slowly on again when he
saw Gilly bearing wide of the dove-cote.

The meadow ended at a field of cut hay. Perhaps it was
there she had her rendezvous, he thought uneasily, and followed even more slowly on the trail of the slight figure flitting
between the ragged lines of haycocks.

He would lose sight of her soon, he realised. She was moving very quickly—so quickly now, in fact that it was clear
she had no intention of lingering in the hayfield either. His
first guess had been wrong after all, Adam decided, but it was
only when he saw Gilly strike off into the rough moorland
running downhill from the hayfield that a further, astonishing

possibility occurred to him.

Gilly might also have decided to investigate the strange light!

If that was so, he concluded, he would kill two birds with one stone, and tease Mistress Gilly afterwards on her new-found daring! Smiling now as he peered ahead, he saw Gilly break into a run through the gorse growing thick on the moor, and speeded his own pace accordingly.

It was rough going through the gorse, for Gilly was only a vague shape flickering like a moth ahead of him and he could not keep her in sight yet still watch his footing. Stones turned under his feet, sharp edges pressing painfully into their bare soles. Branches whipped across his face and caught at his ankles. Inevitably, he stumbled several times, and then fell full length at last. When he scrambled upright again Gilly had vanished from view, and he stood for a moment at a loss to think what his next move should be.

He had drawn level with the light. It was only a few hundred yards away to his left, where the Birsley track rose and fell on its winding course, and it was still keeping close to the line of the track. Its blue glow pulsed and quivered like a living thing in the darkness, and suddenly Adam found he was no longer amused by the thought of Gilly running towards it.

She was a year younger than himself, after all, and she had not a fraction of his strength. If she was too stupid to realise that the light could be dangerous...! He started running again, heading on a straight diagonal that would allow him to intercept the light's twisting path. It was not up to him to protect Gilly of course, he thought as he ran, but it was only sensible to try to stop her before she got a fright that would send her home screaming loud enough to waken the whole household and earn them both a beating.

The ground Adam had to cover now was ridged and dipped like tidal sand sculpted on a giant scale, but his wind was sound and he ran easily with long, rapid strides. The light disappeared from his view in the dips, rose into sight again each time he topped a ridge. Then suddenly he saw Gilly again, a running figure silhouetted briefly against the night-sky. He opened his mouth to call out to her, but some warning instinct forbade noise that might call attention to either of them. He choked back the cry, calculating he still had a chance of catching her before she reached the Birsley track.

The last ridge was behind him before he gave up hope of that chance. Quickly he made for the bushes that marked the line of the Birsley track, and peered as far down its length as he could see. Still there was no sign of Gilly, and he dared not venture out in further search of her now. The light was drawing too close to him. He saw it reflected beyond a turn in the track that masked the source of its glow, and dropped into hiding behind the bushes.

His heart was pounding, but he was vaguely aware of another sound mingling with the drumming of blood in his ears. Hoof-beats! He placed the sound. There was a horse coming down the track towards him, padding softly as if on muffled hooves. Cautiously he looked over the top of the bushes. The horse rounded the turn of the track and his heart lurched with violent, sickening terror at the sight of it.

The horse was aflame; the horse was the source of the light! Head, chest, and flanks all glowed an icy blue, and on hooves like four great balls of blue light it paced forward, carrying a thing as ghastly as itself.

It was neither man nor beast, this thing astride the fiery horse, for its shape was that of a man but its face was a beast's face. The eyes were glowing points of red, the mouth a slit with fangs projecting at either end, the nose was bulged and hooked like an eagle's beak. Two tall horns sprouted from its head, flaring at their tips into an outward curve. The reins the thing clasped to its chest were gripped in great paws that ended in long, cruel-curving talons, and rising from its shoulders were long dragon-wings of leathery black.

The apparition bore down on Adam. His legs gave under him and he slumped to his knees behind the bushes, his mind a confused babble of hymns, prayers, psalms—anything that might save him from the power of the Devil; for the thing riding towards him *was* the Devil. The Reverend Mr. Forrester had thundered its description from the pulpit too often for him to have any doubts on that score!

His flesh shrank. His mind urged flight, but his limbs were powerless to obey. A scream rose into his paralysed throat, and stuck unuttered there. The muffled hoof-beats came nearer.

They drew level with his hiding-place. They were almost on top of him. They were—

They were passing him by!

It was impossible to believe at first. The minutes flowed over Adam as he tried to grasp the fact of his escape, then slowly he raised his head. With a great effort of will he peered beyond the bush-tops, and saw the light from the fiery horse still travelling slowly down the track towards Prestonpans and the sea coast.

It was true then; the Devil had failed to smell him out. He was still whole and unharmed—but oh, dear God, how weak he felt!

Trembling still, Adam dragged himself upright. A whiff of some acrid smell came to his nostrils, and he stiffened in renewed terror. Brimstone! Was that the taint in the air? Mr. Forrester had said that the burning fiery furnace of Hell smelled of brimstone, and that the Devil always brought a whiff of it with him.

Like a goad in his flesh the reminder drove him suddenly into action, running hard to retrace the way he had come. The coarse ground of the moor dropped behind him; the hayfield, the meadow with the high, rounded shape of Seton's dove-cote standing dark in it, then he was running at last along the path skirting the paddock with the gate in the stable-yard wall at the end of it.

The straw in the corner of the outhouse welcomed him. He burrowed into it, gasping in its sweet dry odour, its safe smell of commonplace things, and his heart quietened at last. Yet still his mind continued in turmoil, for at last also he was remembering Gilly.

What had happened to her once she reached the track? Had she also watched from hiding, or had she stood boldly in the open, suspecting no danger from the light? Adam sweated, picturing the Devil suddenly sighting Gilly, urging his horse to a gallop, running her down, engulfing her in blue flame....

With hard, defiant words, he tried to banish the picture from his mind. Gilly meant nothing to him, he reminded himself fiercely. Nobody meant anything to him. That was how he had willed it from the day he had been bound to Seton's service, and he could not afford to soften now at the thought of a silly girl meeting with some mishap.

Yet still the picture of Gilly running from the beast-man on the fiery horse persisted in his mind, and even more gruesome ones crept in beside it—Gilly in the thing's clutches; Gilly's body lying on the track, charred by hell-fire and ripped by talons. Shuddering, he tried to pray again, then stopped, aghast at the words coming from his mouth.

"Our Father which *wert* in heaven..." That was a witch-prayer—the very one the creatures were said to make to their master, the Devil. How had he come to say such a vile thing?

Desperately Adam cast around for some calming thought. Supposing he went to Master Seton in the morning and told him what had happened—or perhaps to Mr. Forrester, the minister? Would either of them believe his story? He was only an orra-lad, the most menial of servants, at everyone's beck and call. Would they take the word of such a one?

They would never believe him, Adam decided. They would say he had invented the story of the Devil to cover up some guilt in Gilly's death, and that might mean a hanging for him!

But supposing he told Master Grahame, the alchemist? There was a thought, now! Adam moved restlessly in his straw, considering the thought from all angles.

Master Grahame was a strange sort of person, of course, and the experiments he was forever making were stranger still. Yet Grahame was still the only person who had ever troubled to show him anything of the world beyond the stable-yard—talking to him, answering his questions, even teaching him to read so that he could make discoveries for himself. Moreover, Grahame had never pried into his thoughts or tried to force friendship on him.

He could trust such a man to keep his confession secret, Adam decided; and surely, if the alchemist believed what he had to say, he would have some advice to offer from the great store of his learning?

Yawning, feeling sleepy at last as hope began to banish some of the horror from his mind, Adam burrowed into the straw again. He would find some opportunity to speak with Master Grahame before anyone could connect him with Gilly's disappearance, he promised himself drowsily, and drifted into a dreamless sleep that lasted till the sky beyond the window-slit was white with the next day's dawn.

"*Gilly!*" was his first thought on wakening, and he hurried out to chop wood for the kitchen fire, wondering what he would say if Mistress Tait, the cook, asked him whether he knew what had become of her kitchenmaid.

Gilly was on her knees cleaning out the fireplace when he brought the wood into the kitchen, and astonishment made him drop his burden to the floor. Gilly looked up, startled by the clatter, and scrambled to her feet, pushing a swathe of straight fair hair back from blue eyes wide with question.

"Gilly! I—I—thought—" Adam advanced a hand uncertainly, doubting the evidence of his own eyes, then suddenly gay with relief he babbled,

"My certes, Gilly, but you gave me a fright! There was I, expecting no harm when I followed you last night—"

"You followed me?" Dismay leapt in Gilly's eyes, but Adam rushed on, too excited to notice it or heed her interruption.

"—and then up started the Devil, and oh, what a grim tyke he was! I near died of fear, I can tell you, when I saw him come riding down Birsley. You should have heard me pray, Gilly; the minister himself could not have rattled the words off faster! Yet still I have been lying awake all night in a fair sweat at the memory of it, and when I saw you just now—"

Adam's chatter broke off abruptly. There were tears in Gilly's eyes, and she was staring in a strangely dazed way at him. The tears spilled down her cheeks, and awkwardly he asked,

"What is't, Gilly? What ails you?"

Gilly raised a hand, dirty with ash from the fire, to dab at the tears. Her fingers shook, leaving a smear of ash on her pale face, and her voice was unsteady also as she said,

"You were foolish to follow me, Adam, for if you speak about it—if you tell anyone what you saw when the Devil was abroad last night, they will kill you."

"*Kill* me? Who? Who will kill me?"

His voice loud with bewilderment and disbelief, Adam advanced on her with the questions, but Gilly turned from him, hiding her face in her hands and crying,

"No, Adam, no ! Do not torment me. I cannot say more— I cannot, I cannot!"

"Gilly, listen—" Adam took her by the shoulders and pulled her round to face him, but she wrenched herself free and backed towards the pantry door. Her features were distorted. Her eyes blazed terror as she hissed,

"Leave me be, leave me be, d'ye hear! I am not wanting to be killed too, for the sake of *your* blabbing tongue!"

She looked as wild and as pitiful as a cat in a trap, Adam thought, and while he stood uneasily staring at her, the sudden appearance of Mistress Tait, the cook, took them both by surprise. Mistress Tait, however, had no eyes for either of them as she swept in from the pantry and let her bulky form slump into a chair by the kitchen table.

Her head was aching, she declared. It had ached from the minute she set foot on the floor that morning, and if she did not have a cold compress for it that moment she would surely die. Groaning, she leaned forward with a hand clasped to her forehead, and from the corner of her eye glimpsed the wood Adam had let fall. Briefly then, she turned a red and angry face to look around her.

"Get that wood stacked, you lazy limmer," she snapped. "And you, Gilly, hurry with that compress."

Adam bent to the wood and Gilly ran for cold water and a napkin. Back at the table she placed the soaked and folded napkin to Mistress Tait's forehead, and glancing up from his work, Adam was relieved to see that she was calm again. There was pity on her face now as she stood listening to Mistress Tait's groans, and after a moment she raised both hands and laid them lightly on the back of the woman's neck.

Gently she began kneading the flesh, her fingers moving skilfully and ever more firmly over it. They were long and very supple fingers, Adam noticed, and was surprised that so slight a creature should have so strong and sure a touch.

"A—a—ah! That's better!" Mistress Tait sighed and arched her neck against the smoothly-working fingers. "Wherever did you learn that trick of easing pain, Gilly?"

"'Tis no trick," Gilly told her quietly. "I have always had healing in my hands."

"What's that you say?" Mistress Tait turned quickly in her chair to fix Gilly with a frowning, uneasy look.

"I have a gift of healing," Gilly replied. "I have always had it."

Mistress Tait's glance slid towards Adam. "Out!" she commanded. "There is plenty of work outside for you, Adam Lawrie."

"Yes, mistress." Adam had to obey, but even although Mistress Tait lowered her harsh voice as he made for the door, he still heard her say warningly,

"For God's sake, girl, be more careful what you say. There are those that would cry deathly harm on you if they heard you claim such a power."

And turning for a last look at Gilly, he saw her shrink away from Mistress Tait with terror returning to distort her face and to blaze again from the wide, staring blue of her eyes.

Chapter 2

THE ALCHEMIST

At the well in the stable-yard, Adam drew water for a morning splash and dried himself with vigorous slapping at his sunburned face and arms; then, shaking back the mop of dark hair clustering damply on his brow, he made for the bothy where the stable-hands ate and slept.

He breakfasted hurriedly there, swallowing his oaten bread and small beer almost untasted as he began to realise how much time he had already wasted that morning, but his haste did not save him. An angry voice calling his name penetrated from the stable-yard and he looked round to see Jardine, the head stable-man, standing in the doorway of the hut.

It was not a pleasant sight. Bad temper gleamed in Jardine's close-set eyes, and pinched his narrow features to an even meaner look. In one hand he carried a wooden measuring-cup, from the fingers of the other dangled a leather bag that chinked as he advanced on Adam.

"Are you deaf as well as stupid, you lousy charity-brat? I have been calling myself hoarse for you."

Lunging viciously on the words he swung the bag of coin, but with the ease of long practice, Adam ducked his head from the blow. Jardine said between his teeth,

"I told you last night you were to fetch salt from Prestonpans this morning. Here—take this!" He tossed over the bag. "And the measure for the coin, too." Sneering, as Adam caught the measuring-cup, he added, "If *I* were Master Seton I would not trust you to pay the salt-panners for me."

"Very likely," Adam retorted. "It takes an honest man to know honesty in others when he sees it."

For answer, Jardine hurled an epithet that brought the blood rushing to Adam's face. Rage leapt into his dark eyes and almost robbed him of breath as he threatened,

"I will make you swallow that yet, Jardine."

Jardine grinned, thin-lipped and yellow-toothed, like a ferret snarling. With the grin growing to a laugh he turned on his heel, and Adam followed him from the hut still tasting rage like bile in his mouth.

The mule-cart for transporting the heavy bags of sea-salt stood ready in the yard. A stable-lad lounged by it, holding the mule's lead-rein. Smiling, his face sly, he tossed the rein to Adam and remarked,

"Y'are late away to the salt-pans, Adam. Jardine has been roaring his head off for you this ten minutes past."

Adam swung up into the cart. Dod Carnegie, he thought, was being civil enough now, but his civility was of very recent date. Glancing down at the stable-hand he answered grimly,

"Aye, Dod. But I will teach Jardine to roar quiet as a mouse one of these days—just as I taught you to roar quiet, not more than a week ago."

Dod half-raised one hand to a bruise still showing under his left eye. His smile going sour, he said,

"Maybe aye, maybe no, Adam Lawrie. Many a cock that crows loud gets its neck wrung all the same."

Without bothering to answer this, Adam urged the mule towards the arched passage-way between the stables and the gable-end of Seton's house, but he was thinking hard as he swung the cart out into the street beyond the passage.

He had always known, of course, that he would have to fight Jardine some day, just as he had fought Dod and all the others who had thought him fair game for their bullying; and now it looked as if that day had come very close. He estimated his chances of winning the fight on Jardine's terms and decided they were not good.

Jardine was ten years older than himself, and wily. Also, he was an expert with cudgels. It would have to be fists, Adam thought, and he would have to take Jardine by surprise for that. Then he would be able to mark that ferret-face—mark it so hard and painfully that even Jardine would at last be forced to join the ranks of those who no longer found it wise to bully the lousy charity-brat! With his face set in hard, determined lines he drove westwards through the village.

School was going in for the day. There were boys racing ahead of him clutching writing-slates to their chests, shirt tails flying as they strove to beat the time of the clanging school bell. Doctor John Fian himself stood at the door of the schoolhouse, his small figure straight as a ruler, cold grey eyes noting every latecomer.

These were the lucky ones, Adam thought enviously; the boys with fathers who could afford to pay blaze-money for candles to light the schoolroom in winter, with a good share left over for the master's fee come Easter Monday. They had not needed to crouch over borrowed books, learning secretly ... He caught the schoolmaster's eye fixed on him and looked uneasily away again.

Fian's gaze remained fixed, and behind the cold pebble-grey of his eyes Fian's brain ticked in cold calculation ... *That was one to watch, that charity-boy with the broad shoulders and hard, alert face. There was a keen mind under that rough thatch of his, a prying mind which could be dangerous....*

"Hup!" Adam brought the rein sharply across the mule's back, and pulled thankfully clear of the schoolhouse. Not that he was afraid of Dr. Fian, of course, he assured himself. But there was talk in the village about him, strange talk that whispered of Fian's learning in magic and other foul arts; and certainly there was something uncanny about the way he stared at a body!

The mule-cart rattled noisily over the jigsaw of stones and summer-dried mud of the roadway. The houses crowding close to it became fewer, and within a few minutes Adam had left the last of the village behind him.

To his right, then, in the shade of some tall beech-trees, he could see the low, barn-like shape of Master Gideon Grahame's house. The sight of it brought sharp recollection of his resolve to seek the alchemist's advice, and with Gilly's strange little warning ringing again in his ears he turned the mule on to the path leading to the front door. Grahame's voice answered his knock, calling him to enter, and he stepped through the doorway into the single long room that served the alchemist for living-quarters and workshop combined.

Master Grahame was seated at the desk in the centre of

the room, quill-pen in hand, shabby velvet skull cap askew on the luxuriant mass of his grey hair. He raised dark, deep-set eyes at Adam's entrance, smiled, and said absently, "Aye, Adam," before bending again to his writing.

He had just finished another of his experiments, Adam guessed. The furnace at one end of the room was still glowing. There were several books lying open on the great four-poster bed at the room's opposite end, and the work-bench under the window behind the desk was littered with all the various implements of his profession.

For a moment or two he stood watching the swift movement of the alchemist's pen, then turned to scan the shelves that lined the wall facing the window. Idly he moved along them studying the titles of the books that competed for space there with jars and phials of chemicals, then lifted a book from its place and began to read. Grahame glanced up, covertly noting his choice.

The hard lines of Adam's face relaxed as he read, and the alchemist smiled again, noting this also. His attention wandered further from the papers on his desk, back to the day he had surprised a boy peering through the window of his workshop—a small and dirty boy who had returned him scowl for scowl, yet had still obstinately held his ground until he had been given answers to all the questions he had to ask.

That was only a little more than five years ago, Grahame calculated, but five years is a long time in a boy's life and Adam had learned a great deal since then. As for himself... His smile fading, he glanced back to the notes of his experiment.

They had been a wasted five years, he decided; as wasted as all the others he had spent buried in this ignorant country backwater where the gentry despised him for a charlatan, the minister damned his experiments for impious meddling with God's natural order, and the other inhabitants jeered at him for a madman. And yet this was where he had spent half his lifetime now!

It had been a high price to pay for the name and the face God had given him—thirty years of exile from the intellectual life of the city, from the interest of patrons at Court, even from the companionship of his own profession; too high a price, he decided moodily. Yet what choice had he but to pay, and go on paying till he died? Sighing, he gave up the attempt to concentrate on his notes, and rose from his desk.

Adam was too engrossed in his book to notice the movement, and for a moment the alchemist studied him, aware suddenly that he was seeing a boy at a turning point in his life. It had been some compensation for his own wasted years, he supposed, to have taught something to this most teachable of boys. But what of the years that Adam might waste? There would have to be some crack in his armour soon, some softening of his defiant attitude to the rest of the world. Otherwise, the sullen, friendless boy was almost certainly doomed to a lonelier and even more embittered manhood.

It was time he accepted some responsibility for preventing that, Grahame decided, but he would go very cautiously at first or Adam would simply retire even further behind his defences. Quietly he approached the bookshelves. Still Adam did not look up from his book, and touching him lightly on the shoulder Grahame remarked,

"I did not waste my time, it seems, when I taught you to read."

Adam looked up. The lines of his face hardened again, and bluntly he answered,

"I sometimes wonder why you bothered to do so."

Grahame shrugged. "You have a good mind—too good to be wasted in ignorance, and it pleasured me to teach you. Forbye, there is no man can live entirely to himself, as you will learn sooner or later to your cost, my friend."

"Maybe I will." Adam closed the book and put it carefully back into place, then faced Grahame again. "But meantime, Master Grahame, 'tis the only way of enduring my kind of life without being trodden underfoot."

"As you wish, Adam." Shrugging in dismissal this time, Grahame turned back to his desk and seated himself again. "Tell me how I can serve you this morning."

"I am not sure." Adam frowned, wondering what he should say, and followed Grahame to the desk. "A strange thing has happened to me, Master Grahame," he went on slowly. "Last night I saw the Devil."

"You what?" Grahame looked up, startled, from arranging

the skirts of his long black robe around his knees.

"I saw the Devil, sir," Adam repeated. "I saw him riding down Birsley Brae on a fiery horse."

He looked sharply at Grahame, half-expecting to see him smile, but found nothing except wary attention on his face. So far, so good, he thought, and began telling his story in a more orderly manner.

Grahame continued to listen intently, leaning back in his chair and occasionally rasping the fingers of one long white hand across his chin. He made no comment, and his expression did not change until Adam came to speak of his horror at the thought of Gilly's fate. A look of impatience crossed his face then, and he said sharply,

"But this Gilly Duncan suffered no harm. You have discovered that since, have you not?"

"Yes, sir," Adam admitted. "I saw her this morning, looking as usual."

"And you are absolutely sure you saw this—this apparition?"

"Absolutely sure," Adam repeated. "I only wish I had never followed Gilly last night." He looked uneasily at Grahame. "Do you not believe I saw the Devil, sir?"

"H'mm?" Grahame's thoughts had been wandering, and he recalled himself with difficulty. "Yes—yes, of course I believe you, Adam. Now listen. Have you spoken to anyone else about this?"

"Only to Gilly," Adam told him, and Grahame pounced on the answer.

"How much did you tell her?"

"Why—" Adam hesitated, taken aback by the sharpness of the question. "I did not get a chance to say much, sir; only that I had followed her and had seen the Devil. Gilly was very frightened to hear that, but when I tried to discover the reason for her fear, she behaved strangely to me. *If you speak about it,* she said, *if you tell anyone what you saw when the Devil was abroad last night, they will kill you.* And so I came to ask your advice, sir. I thought—"

Grahame did not wait to hear what Adam had thought. Rising abruptly, he began pacing the room, a name from the past ringing suddenly loud in his mind and bringing long-buried memory to life again. Silently, with bitter anger as he paced, he cursed the name and cursed the fate that had sent it to haunt him again; yet knew still with hopeless certainty that he was facing a ghost which could never be laid. But how explain that to the boy who had raised it? Adam's wondering face caught his eye as he slowed in his long, restless stride, and halted by the window.

A sharp warning was needed, even sharper than the one Gilly had given; but how much could he safely tell Adam? He could not betray that name—that cursed name that was still so dear to him; yet it was essential to put the boy well on his guard. Moreover, Adam was curious, and he had too sharp a mind to be easily deceived. He would have to be told enough of the truth to satisfy that curiosity.

Head bent, hands clasped behind his back, Grahame stood arranging what he would say. With his gaunt height hunched thus into his long robe of dusty black, he had the forlorn look of some solitary old crow, yet still Adam dared not break the silence his stillness imposed. He waited, wondering at the other's dejected appearance, and eventually the alchemist spoke in a voice so low he had to strain to hear it.

"How much do you know about witchcraft, Adam?"

"Witchcraft!" Startled, Adam turned the word over. "Why, nothing, sir. How could I know anything of that?"

"How, indeed!" Grahame turned towards him, his long face impassive now and voice returned to its normal pitch. "Witchcraft is a secret pursuit. Yet it is widely practised in this country, and if you wish to understand the warning Gilly gave you, I must first explain something of it. But do not try to question me on how I came by my knowledge of witch affairs, for that lies so close to my heart that I cannot speak of it—not now, at least. Not now!"

Distress quivered suddenly in Grahame's face again. Adam held his breath for fear of disturbing further revelations, and quickly mastering his features the alchemist continued,

"First of all then, Adam, you must understand how the witches direct their activities. The leading spirits among them are formed into bands of thirteen, called 'covens', and each group of covens has a Grand Master to preside over its meetings. These meetings are called 'Esbats', and the lesser sort of witch is not allowed to attend them.

"But four times a year, on the eve of each of the great festivals of Candlemass, Beltane, Lammas, and Hallowmass, *all* the witches of a district gather to hold the meeting called 'Grand Sabbat'; and last night, you will recall, was the 31st of July—Lammas Eve. Last night, every witch in Tranent, in Prestonpans, Longniddry. and all the other villages around here, was present at the Grand Sabbat of Lammas."

Grahame paused, his face setting into hard, tight lines. "And that, Adam," he finished, "was how you happened to see the Devil ride forth; for it is the Devil himself who always presides over the Grand Sabbat of the witches."

Adam felt the hair prickle on the back of his neck. Breathlessly he asked, "And Gilly? Why did she say *They will kill you?*"

Grahame eyed him sombrely. "She must have jumped to the conclusion that you knew about the Sabbat and had spied on it also, or she would not have voiced such a warning. And believe me, Adam, it is one you must treat seriously, for the witches certainly have the power to kill and they would not hesitate to use it on anyone who betrayed their secrets."

It was all very hard to believe, Adam thought. He stared at the alchemist, striving to take in the full meaning of his words, and was suddenly incredulous of the fantastic picture they painted.

"But, sir," he protested, "all those villages you named are such quiet places, and their people have always seemed so God-fearing. Who could be witches among them?"

"Think!" Grahame urged softly, and Adam thought, recalling names, faces, scraps of gossip....

"Doctor Fian!" he exclaimed, and Grahame nodded.

"Very likely," he agreed, "and you could soon name others if you tried. But keep such names to yourself, and whatever you do, say nothing to anyone of what you saw last night or they may leap to the same conclusion as Gilly did. And one last warning. Say nothing more of this to Gilly herself; but watch her, Adam. Watch her closely from now on, or she could be a real danger to you."

"Very well, sir, if you think it wise," Adam agreed, "but—" He hesitated, frowning over his thoughts, then puzzled aloud,

"Gilly is not much more than a child, after all, and so timid she is frightened of her own shadow. How could she have known about the Sabbat in the first place?"

"Oh, Adam," Grahame groaned in exasperation, "you are simple! There is only one way she could have known about it, of course. She was there—she was one of them! Your timid little Gilly is also a witch."

Chapter 3

ALL FOR A WITCH

The fight with Jardine happened suddenly, giving Adam no opportunity to choose either his ground or his tactics; and Gilly Duncan was the cause of it.

She came out into the stable-yard with a yoke of buckets about her neck, and went to the well. Adam was seated on the wood-pile, mending a bridle, and he watched as she unyoked herself and lowered the first of the buckets into the well. It was late in the afternoon some two weeks after his visit to the alchemist. The yard was quiet, except for faint cries coming from the hayfield where Jardine had taken two of Master Seton's hounds to course hares.

Gilly looked very frail, struggling to lift the full bucket from the well, but Adam resisted the thought of helping her. Let her fight her own battles, he thought grimly. He had been frail enough, too, when he was bound to Master Seton's service, but no-one had lifted a finger to help him. And besides, why should he do anything for a witch?

Gilly lowered the bucket to the ground and stayed bent over it, fighting to catch her breath. There was a flash of movement at the open gate in the stable-yard wall—a blur of brown that became a hare flying full stretch across the stable-yard.

It circled, finding no way out; then after the manner of its kind, doubled on its tracks and took refuge. Gilly had not straightened, or moved from her position, and the place it chose was the shadowy hollow in the long, sweeping folds of her gown.

Still Gilly did not move, but as the cries from the hayfield grew louder, she reached out her hands. Slowly she reached, and gently her hands slipped under the body of the crouched hare. Slowly and gently she lifted it, and straightened up, holding it cradled against her.

The beast should have struggled; it should have leapt free, should even have screamed, as hares do in extremity of terror: but it did none of these things and Adam watched, dumbfounded, as it lay quiet and quivering in Gilly's arms.

Jardine's voice was close now. Adam's eyes met Gilly's, knowing there could be only seconds to spare before the hunt arrived in the stable-yard. His own voice hoarse with urgency he blurted,

"Put it down!"

Gilly shook her head, and the hounds burst into the stable-yard. Long, lean, and yelping with excitement they rushed straight for her, but swiftly she threw her apron up to cover the hare and backed against the parapet of the well.

"Put it down! Put it down!"

This time it was Jardine, yelling as he ran through the gateway and saw the hounds leaping and snapping at the bundle in Gilly's arms.

Gilly clung tightly to it, but now the hare was struggling. With a sweep of his arm, Jardine knocked it out of her grip, and the hounds were on it, tearing it between them, and Gilly's screams were mingling with the screams of the dying hare.

Adam found himself on his feet, one shaking hand clenched tightly round the half-mended bridle. Jardine kicked the hare's carcase across the yard, and the snarling hounds at Gilly's feet leapt after it. Gilly slumped down against the well's parapet, but Jardine gripped her by the shoulder and pulled her upright again. His lean features twisted with anger, he told her,

"Interfere with a man's sport, heh! I'll teach you, you stupid besom. I'll teach you!"

A slap on the cheek with the flat of his hand followed, a slap on the other cheek with the back of his hand. Gilly's head jerked with each blow. She stared dumbly at Jardine, offering no resistance.

She should be clawing at Jardine's eyes, kicking his shins, tearing his hair. Adam thought desperately. Even Jardine would back down from the kind of retaliation an angry female could offer, but still Gilly was sagging brokenly in his grip, and still he was slapping her back and forward, and the marks of his fingers were branded red on her white face.

Adam did not realise that he had leaped forward, or that he was growling like an animal as he pushed Gilly away with one hand and swung the bridle with the other. The metal bit of the bridle caught Jardine high on the cheekbone and blood sprang brightly from a line of broken skin. Jardine recoiled, roaring with pain and astonishment, and Adam swung again.

Now he was fully aware of his actions and the consequences they would have. Jardine had not attacked him. He had attacked Jardine, and there could be no escaping the punishment that would bring. With the savagery of despair he swung the bridle again, and had the satisfaction of hearing Jardine roar with pain again as he staggered and clutched at a red weal rising on his neck.

Adam shortened his grip on the bridle. Jardine snatched a wood-strake from the pile near the well and whirled round, swinging it like a cudgel. Adam lashed out at its descending stroke, missed his aim, and the cudgel took him heavily across the shoulders. He pitched forward. Jardine's booted foot came up to meet his face. He caught it, and heaved, and they fell together in a bellowing tangle.

Adam was first on his feet, dropping the bridle as he rose. Fists clenched, head down, he rushed in under the swing of Jardine's cudgel, and managed a double strike at his already-damaged cheekbone. Jardine fenced him off with the cudgel held like a bar before his chest, and kicked again. Adam twisted to avoid the kick, and in the same movement grasped the bar, jerking Jardine towards himself. His free hand travelled up and forward, taking Jardine squarely in the right eye, but the blow unbalanced him, and before he could recover his stance Jardine was laying into him with the cudgel.

Arms raised to protect his head, Adam staggered under the blows watching his chance, and saw it as Jardine raised the cudgel high for the blow that would break his guard. He sprang, putting every ounce of effort into his leap. His right hand closed on the descending cudgel, his left shoulder thrust hard against Jardine's chest, his forehead crashed against Jardine's mouth.

They went down together again, a weakened Jardine fighting for possession of the cudgel and swearing incoherently through the blood streaming from his mouth. It was all over bar the shouting, Adam exulted fiercely, and felt a whip like a red-hot stroke laid across his back. The hem of a fur-trimmed gown swung before his eyes, and he rolled over, relaxing his grip on Jardine.

Master Seton was towering over him, Master Seton in the cocked hat and fur-trimmed robe of his office as Baillie of the Town Council, and it was Master Seton's whip that had been laid across him.

"On your feet, both of you!"

Seton's voice cracked as sharply as his whip. The hand that held the reins of the horse he had ridden into the stable-yard was knuckled white with anger, and his little, close-set eyes blazed like chips of fire from his fleshy face.

"You!" he commanded Jardine. "Speak first!"

"The kitchenmaid—that thrawn besom, Gilly—tried to stop the hounds coursing a hare. I slapped her face for her, and this—" Jardine spat blood with a fragment of tooth in it, and glared venomously at Adam. "—this gallows' scum here attacked me."

The red, fleshy face swung round to Adam. "Is that true, Adam Lawrie? You struck first at Jardine?"

"Yes, sir," Adam admitted. "It is true I struck first, but—"

"I will have no 'buts'," Seton roared. "I am a Baillie of the Town Council, boy. I know the law, and the law recognises only plain, straightforward facts."

He turned to Jardine again. "Jardine, I will be plain with you. It is a serious offence for a bond-servant to attack a free man to his injury, and you could bring such a charge against Adam Lawrie in the Sheriff Court. But that would lose me a good workman if the Sheriff condemns him to prison, or to hanging. Will you be content for me to deal with him under my authority as Baillie? I promise you he will be soundly punished."

"Well, sir..." Jardine hesitated, then quailed under the glare in Seton's eye and changed his tone to one of fawning deference. "Indeed, sir, I am content. I know you will see justice done, Master Seton."

"Good!" Seton swung round and caught sight of a curious face peering from the stable. "You! Dod Carnegie!" he roared. "Bind this fellow's hands and take him along at my horse's tail to the House of Correction."

"Yes, sir." Dod's face vanished for a moment. As he re-appeared from the stable carrying a rope, Seton said,

"You can take my note of instruction to the Town Con-stable, Jardine. Come!'

He was off in a swirl of red robe. Jardine trailed after him, triumphant malice gleaming on his battered features. Dod Carnegie came forward, grinning, and grinned the wider as he saw Adam's glance searching around for Gilly.

"You were a fool to play hero for that one," he said spite-fully. "She was off like a flash of lightning the minute the fight started."

Of course he had been a fool, Adam thought bitterly. If he had fought Jardine on his own account as he had planned to do, he could have let him get in the first blow and then pleaded self-defence. As it was. . . . He shrugged the thought away and recalled Jardine's bruised and bleeding face to mind. That was one consolation to take with him to the House of Correction. He had kept his vow to mark Jardine, and with a face like that to remind him it would be a while before he tried any of his bullying tricks again.

Stumbling through the streets at the tail of Seton's horse, Adam kept this thought firmly before him. In the House of Correction, lying face down with his hands secured through the slots in the birching-table, he concentrated grimly on it, but felt it slip away from him with the first sting of the birch-rod across his back.

Setting his teeth against the pain of the rod descending on him again, and yet again, he drew on every ounce of his courage to endure without crying out, until he lost count of the strokes at last and slid over the edge of consciousness with Jardine and pain and courage all mixed up in his mind, and none of them seeming to matter any more.

It was impossible to lie still enduring the pain of his wounds; impossible to move without fresh agony as his shirt pulled free of the blood crusted into it. And it was all for a witch, this fiery pain; all for the sake of a crazy creature who could make a hare lie still in her arms, yet would not defend herself against a slapping as any sensible maid would have done.

Lying face down in the outhouse, where Jardine and Dod Carnegie had tossed him, Adam clenched his fists in a fury of resentment, and groaned as the movement sent more pain stabbing up his back.

"Adam . . . !"

The voice was soft, only a little above a whisper. The straw of his bed rustled to some movement other than his own. Adam lay still, every muscle suddenly tense, till the voice came again softly repeating his name. He raised his head then and said harshly,

"Go away. Get back to your own place, Gilly Duncan."

"But I came to help you. You fought for me. 'Tis the least I can do now."

The straw rustled again as Gilly dropped to her knees beside him. He turned his head slowly, painfully. He had no idea how long he had lain there, but now it was dark outside and Gilly's face was only a pale blur above him. Grimly he told the pale face,

"I fought because I lost my temper, and that would not have happened if you had had the wit to stand up for yourself—"

"I was too frightened of Jardine," Gilly interrupted breathlessly, but he bore on over her words,

"—but after the first blow, I fought on my own behalf— as I always do. And so now will you go? You owe me nothing, and I want no help from you."

For answer, Gilly threw back her cloak and set down the lantern she had been hiding under it. She had a pitcher of water and a piece of linen in her other hand, and still without speaking, she began gently to bathe Adam's shirt away from the blood that made it cling to his skin.

"Lie still!" she told him when he protested again and tried to push away her hand. Her face was intent, purposeful, and her tone was crisp. She was suddenly very sure of herself, Adam thought, and somehow it was too much of an effort to argue further with her. Nor could he offer any more physical resistance. The pain of movement was too intense for that.

He lay still, yielding his tenseness to the soothing touch of warm water as Gilly eased his shirt free and gently washed the dried blood from his wounds.

"I have brought you a clean one," she said quietly, laying the soiled shirt to one side, "and I have a powder here that will have your wounds all healed by the morning."

Adam looked up to see her reaching into the pocket of her gown, and frowned at the little box she withdrew from it.

"I have never heard of a powder that heals in a night," he said suspiciously, and Gilly nodded.

"Aye, likely," she agreed, "but I have receipts for cures that no-one else has. My mother taught them to me, and she had great knowledge of herbs and all kinds of physic. This one is a sure way to promote rapid healing."

She was sprinkling the powder on his back as she spoke, and he twisted his head around to watch her. The movement sent little stabs of pain across his back again, but the fierce, the overwhelming pain of his wounds had subsided; and, he realised, his resentment at Gilly had died with it. He sat up awkwardly, reaching to take the clean shirt she handed him when she had finished dusting the powder on his back, and Gilly gathered up her cloth and pitcher as he put the shirt on.

"You will be able to sleep now," she told him, and picked up her lantern. Adam fumbled for some expression of thanks, but no words came. Gilly made to rise from her knees, and he said impulsively,

"No—wait! Wait a moment, Gilly."

She waited, her face pale and still in the lantern's pale light, her eyes fixed expectantly on him. She was a witch, the alchemist had claimed, and in his resentment at the pain he had suffered because of her he had cursed her for such a creature. *Watch her closely*, the alchemist had warned, and for two weeks now he had watched her. But to what purpose?

She had not lied about her healing powers. He had discovered that easily enough from old Davy Denholm, the ploughman at Netherholm, who claimed that the mere touch of her hands had cured him of fever. And there was the carrier who brought mail for Seton from Edinburgh, and who said she had cured his rheumatism with physic and more laying-on of hands. But did that prove she was a witch?

Perhaps not—but what about her visits to Dr. Fian? Adam shifted uneasily under Gilly's stare, remembering how she had twice visited Dr. Fian in the past two weeks; slipping out to his house the first time when everyone else in the Seton household was taking a Sabbath afternoon rest, and the other time at night when they were all asleep. All except for himself, Adam thought, and both times he had watched for her leaving the house because she had seemed as nervous as a cat for hours beforehand.

More than nervous, he corrected himself. She had been frightened; even more frightened than she ordinarily was of people like Jardine. Yet if Dr. Fian was a witch and she was a witch too, why should she fear him? And moreover, she was so young for such evil. How *could* she be a witch?

Gilly was still waiting for him to speak, her eyes fixed on his face, hands folded in her lap. Her meekness irritated him, and abruptly he demanded,

"Are you a witch, Gilly?"

Gilly's stare widened. Her lips began to tremble and she stammered, "You—you must not ask such a question."

"A hare is a witch's creature," Adam persisted. "Is that why the one that escaped the hounds lay quiet in your arms?"

Unexpectedly, Gilly smiled. "No, you are wrong there. I can gentle any creature—I always could. They trust me, I think, and there is something about my touch that quietens them."

"That could be, I suppose," Adam conceded. "But what about the night I followed you? I ran from the Devil then, but you ran towards him; towards a witch-meeting. Is that not true?"

"I will not answer you." Gilly looked away from him her lips trembling again. "I cannot answer such questions."

"But I say you must," Adam told her, "because if you are a witch you are a great fool, for you run the risk of being burnt in the justice-fire, and—"

"And it is talk like that that will get me burnt!" Sharply Gilly interrupted him, then clapped her hand to her mouth in panic as she realised what she had said.

"You see!" Adam accused. "You have just admitted the charge."

"You trapped me into it," Gilly cried. "But I never wanted to be a witch, I never wanted that!"

"Then why?" Perplexed, Adam stared at her, then coaxed, "Tell me why, Gilly. I will keep your confidence, never fear for that."

"You promise?" With fear and doubt in her eyes, Gilly stared back at him, and before he could answer added uncertainly, "I—I have longed so often to tell someone. If I thought I could trust you . . ."

"You can trust me," Adam assured her. "I swear I will say nothing to betray you. I swear it on the Holy Bible."

Gilly swallowed hard, and braced herself as if for some ordeal. Tensely she said, "Then I will tell you why, and you will see I am speaking the truth." She looked away from him gathering her thoughts together and then went on,

"It began in my childhood. I was brought up on a little farm a few miles from here, near the village of Keith. My parents were both good to me, but they did not agree with one another, and when I was ten years old my father thrust my mother out of the house. She took me with her and we stayed with Mistress Agnes Sampson of Keith until my mother died, about three months ago. That was when Mistress Sampson found me employment here."

She paused, looking down at her hands as if the rest of her story lay there. Adam waited silently, guessing that the important part of it was yet to come, and eventually Gilly said,

"Mistress Sampson is a witch, Adam. My mother was a witch too, and that was the cause of my father's quarrel with her. Now are you answered?"

Adam shook his head, frowning. "You will have to speak plainer than that, Gilly."

Gilly leaned towards him. Her lantern-lit eyes had a feverish brilliance now, and her voice shook as she asked,

"Do you not know that a witch mother commonly vows her infant to the Devil, just as a Christian mother vows her infant to God? And that the witch mother takes her child to the Devil to confirm that vow, just as the Christian mother takes her child to church for Holy Confirmation?"

"No," Adam shook his head, gazing with fascinated horror into the brilliant eyes fixed on him. "I did not know that."

"Then you are lucky," Gilly told him bitterly, "for that was what happened to me, Adam. On the day I was born, my mother vowed me to the Devil, and took me with her to my first witch-meeting to confirm that vow. I was eleven years old then, and small for my age, so that the Devil laughed to see me. *What shall I do with such a little bird as she?* he asked my mother. Then he told me, *Bow down, Gilly Duncan, and I will make you mine.* And because there was no help for it, I bowed down and did him the homage that all witches do. Then the Devil pricked my shoulder with a sharp thing like a bodkin that left a blue mark on my skin, and so signed me to his covenant and made a witch of me."

Gilly's voice died into silence, and all the life in her seemed to die with it. Her head drooped. She slumped, slack and dispirited, and Adam felt his horror at her story changing gradually to impatience.

"Listen, Gilly," he told her. "You do not have to be a witch if you do not want to be one. No-one has to be bound to another's will."

"You are bound to Seton," Gilly said dully.

"Aye," Adam nodded, "my service is bound to him. But not my will! That will always be my own."

"What do you mean by that?" Gilly looked up, a spark of interest returning to her eyes, and Adam held her look with his own.

"I mean this," he said grimly. "My father was a farmer too, but he was bankrupted by harsh laws, then hanged for stealing some of his own corn to feed me; and my mother was hanged alongside him for art and part in his crime. I was only a little lad then, and I stood at the foot of the scaffold bawling my eyes out, until Master David Seton claimed me for his bond-servant —as any worthy citizen has the right to do with a felon's child.

"I stopped crying then, and kicked Seton—kicked him with all my might, and I have gone on in that way ever since. Now there are few who dare to bully me, for I fight back against them all. I yield my will to nobody, Gilly, and it could be the same for you if you would only learn to fight back against the witches."

"No." Gilly shook her head. "It is not so simple as that, Adam. Not for me, anyway."

She rose to her feet, putting out a hand to silence his further protest. "Wait," she told him. "There is something else you should know. One of us suspects you, Adam. He has no grounds for doing so, except that he knows you have an enquiring mind and so is afraid you may discover something through me. Well, now you have, *and you must treat it as a warning of the witches' power.* Do you hear?"

Fian! She is talking about Fian, Adam thought. *That is why she has been slipping out to see him!*

Aloud, he said, "I told you. I will not talk." Rising to follow her movement to the door, he added, "And I am grateful for your physic, Gilly."

"Then say nothing of that either," she warned. "The less there is to connect you with me, the better it will be for both of us." And without waiting to hear any further reply, glided quickly away across the stable-yard.

Adam watched her go, his mind churning with such a medley of thoughts that he quite failed to notice a slight movement in the shadow of the stable-hands' bothy. Nor did he hear the faint scuffle of Jardine's feet as he moved cautiously back into deeper hiding.

Chapter 4

ESBAT

August had brought harvest weather with it, and an end to the cold wind from the sea, but the spell of warm, still days ran on for too long. Thunder began to build up in the air. The noon sky shimmered with heat-haze. The evenings dragged by under masses of sulky, lead-coloured cloud, and still the storm they threatened did not break. By mid-September, day and night alike were stifling and Adam found himself watching the sky impatiently, yet with growing uneasiness.

It was not only the knowledge of the storm to come that was affecting him, however, he admitted to himself. All his thoughts nowadays seemed to be uneasy ones, and working one day to stack Master Seton's hay before the storm could scatter it, he tried to pin down the reasons for this.

First of all, there was Jardine. A lot of the bluster had gone out of him since the day of the fight and he had not attempted any more bullying; but there was something sinister in his new quietness. Those ferrety eyes had taken on a very watchful look, Adam thought, and wondered if Jardine was hoping to catch him out in something that would merit yet another whipping. He was a spiteful creature, after all, and it would be just like him to want a double helping of revenge.

Then there was Master Grahame, who had warned him to watch Gilly and had not been at all pleased with evasive answers to his questions about that watch. Yet how was it possible to keep his promise of silence over Gilly's confession and still be honest with Master Grahame?

And of course, there was Gilly herself, who might as well be dumb nowadays for all that she said to anyone. But there had been one occasion, Adam recalled uneasily, when she had spoken to him and he had wished it otherwise.

They had been coming back from market together, carrying Mistress Tait's heavy basket of purchases between them, and Gilly had caught his attention with a sudden gasp and a jerk of her head towards one of the market-stalls.

"There! Look over there," she whispered. "The big woman —that is Mistress Agnes Sampson."

Adam looked and saw a tall, heavily-built woman with features that seemed too small for her big, round face, but this defect apart, she seemed ordinary enough. Her dress was quiet and dignified, and the yellow-starched ruff round her neck showed that she could afford to follow the fashions. Anything less like a witch, in fact, was hard to imagine, and perhaps Gilly had seen the look of doubt on his face for she whispered,

"You would not think it to look at her, would you, that she has made ointments from the flesh of unchristened babes?"

With a quick shudder of revulsion Adam recalled the words, and then remembered how Gilly's voice had trembled as she spoke. But that was no concern of his, he told himself. Gilly must go to hell in her own way now that she had refused to listen to him, and it might not be long before she took her first step on the road to the justice-fire, for now he was not the only one who had noticed her nervousness. Mistress Tait had begun to look oddly at her too, and there was nothing he could do about that—except maybe to warn her to grease the hinges of the kitchen door.

Three times now he had heard it squeaking as she opened it cautiously for more of her night-prowling, but sooner or later someone else was bound to hear it, and then... A large, warm drop of rain splashing on to the back of his neck startled him into realising how close the storm had come to breaking, and putting all his problems to one side for the moment he re-doubled his efforts to get the hay stacked before the light failed.

The storm broke an hour later in a crash of thunder that released a brief but heavy rain-burst. The lull that followed lasted till darkness set in, then the thunder rolled again, far-off to begin with but coming closer with each peal.

Crouched in his straw with the doorless entrance to the

outhouse framing his view, Adam watched the lightning's wild pattern flashing over the sky, and counted the seconds between each flash and the thunder-clap that followed. It was a night for all decent Christians to be a-bed, a real witches' night, he thought, glancing uneasily towards the kitchen door; and was not surprised a little later when it opened to let Gilly's small figure slip cautiously into the yard.

Silently she made for the arched passage-way leading to the street beyond the house, and a sudden fascination with the purpose of her excursion gripped Adam. Was she indeed bound for a witch-meeting? If so, what sights might not be witnessed on such an occasion, on such a night! Like a sleep-walker drawn from his bed by the horrid compulsion of a dream, he rose and stealthily followed her stealthy progress into the street.

The village lay asleep in a dark huddle of twisted roofs and tip-tilted gables, with rain-washed alleys wound into the heart of the huddle. In the High Street also, where starlight gleamed fitfully on wet cobble-stones, there was no ring of footsteps. No light showed through the chinks of its shuttered windows, but at the end of the street where the schoolhouse stood, Adam made out the shape of a horse and rider.

Instantly he slipped into the shadow of a doorway, and froze there watching Gilly hurry on towards the mounted man. He was evidently expecting her, for he raised a hand in salute to her approaching figure. Gilly broke into a run. The horseman leaned sideways in his saddle, stretching the hand out to her, and when she was near enough to grasp it he swung her up to sit astride the crupper of his horse. Turning the beast's head then, he rode off, and Adam stepped out of hiding to take up the trail again.

It would be a simple enough matter now, he reckoned, for now he could keep a fair distance behind the horse and rely on the sound of its hoof-beats to guide him. Running silently past the last few houses of the village he speculated on the identity of the horseman, and guessed at Dr. Fian. The place of rendezvous outside the schoolhouse fitted with such a guess, he argued, and so did what he already knew of Gilly. And if he was right in one thing he was almost certainly right in the other; for where could these two be headed except to a witches' meeting?

The horseman was riding west, but within a few minutes he made a sharp right-hand turn on to the Birsley track winding northwards towards the sea. He had put his mount to a canter, and for brief seconds as he followed its swift movement Adam saw his quarry illumined by the lightning still flashing across the sky. The peak of the storm could not be far off now, he guessed, and wondered at the hardihood of the witches. But then, perhaps they themselves had raised the storm!

With vague memories of having heard that witches could do such a thing, he ducked his head nervously from the thunderclap that followed the flash. Running downhill over the slippery mud of the track had its own risks, however, and he had to watch sharply for the moving shape ahead of him. Impatiently he shrugged off such fancied fears, and concentrated his whole mind on the pursuit down Birsley.

At the foot of the track lay Prestonpans, huddled as dark in sleep as his own village had been, but Fian was not making for Prestonpans itself. He swung left just before he came to it, and rode westwards along the outskirts of the village until the track he had taken petered out into wasteland. The soft ground absorbed his horse's hoofbeats, so that Adam no longer had any sound to guide him, and beyond the wasteland lay high sand-dunes that would soon conceal his quarry from view. Instinctively he made a spurt to close the gap between them, but quickly checked his headlong pace in favour of more cautious action.

The sand-dunes, he knew, formed a horse-shoe shape framing the tiny fishing-harbour of Aitchison's Haven; and between the harbour jetty and the first wave of dunes was a flat, grassy patch of ground where the fishermen were accustomed to dry their nets. That, he decided, was the only place that could possibly hold any sort of gathering, and so that was almost certainly Fian's destination. What he had to do now, therefore, was to find some point from which he could overlook the space enclosed by the dunes, and quickly making his choice he ran towards the seaward tip of one side of the horse-shoe.

There was cover for him at the point he had chosen, for the upper slopes of the dunes were heavily over-grown with long, coarse-leaved rushes. Crouching low, with the fine white sand of the dunes slipping away from under him with every movement, he clawed his way up to the rushy growth on the highest dune, then flat on his belly wriggled on through the jungle of thick stems. A sound of voices drifted up to him as he reached the top of the dune, and carefully parting the stems before his face, he looked down from his vantage point.

To his right lay the harbour with its usual clutter of small boats rocking at anchor. On his left was the flat grassy ground where the fishermen pegged out their nets, and it was from this space enclosed by the horse-shoe of dunes that the voices came. There were people grouped there, both men and women. He counted their number, and the figure he reached made him pause to check his count. The figure remained the same and with a curious inward trembling he realised what it meant.

Thirty-nine—three times thirteen; if the alchemist had been right in what he said, there were three covens of witches gathered there below him now!

It was a very restless gathering, he realised also. Groups kept forming from the general mass and breaking up again, and every so often there were louder words breaking through their low-voiced conversation. A clap of thunder sounding almost directly overhead made him wince suddenly, and glancing up to the torn and livid sky he wondered if the witches were arguing over something, or whether it was the storm itself that was making them so restless.

A single voice calling out peremptorily brought Adam's gaze back to the hollow in the dunes. One man, he saw, was marshalling the witches into a form of order; a short, sparely-built man who pointed his directions with a long wand that gleamed white in the dimness of the hollow. The voice, the figure, the schoolmasterish manner made him unmistakably Dr. Fian, but Adam found no relish in seeing all his guesswork thus confirmed. He searched for Gilly among the witches forming the wide circle Dr. Fian commanded, and cursed soundlessly as a figure smaller and slighter than the others caught his eye.

What a fool she was—what a fool to let some childhood

promise bind her to this evil crew! What a fool to travel so blindly on the road to the justice-fire—and worse, the fearful eternal fires of hell!

Now Dr. Fian was standing at the centre of the witches' circle. He raised the long slim wand high, and their voices hushed. The wand moved, its tip tracing a strange and complicated design upon the darkness, and wild as a seagull wailing Dr. Fian's voice rose suddenly in the first line of a chanted litany:

"Secretum secretorum! Secretum secretorum! Secretum secretorum!"

"Tu operans sis secretus horum!"

The massed voices of the witches wailed in response, and although the words were so much gibberish to Adam, the sound of them sent prickles of horror down his spine.

Dr. Fian chanted the next line of his litany, his wand tracing a design again as he chanted. The witches chanted in reply; and now they danced, facing outwards from the centre of the circle, neighbour's arms close-linked round neighbour's shoulders and the circle turning anti-clockwise.

Louder, faster Dr. Fian chanted, and faster drew his strange shapes on the dark air. Louder, faster, the witches responded, and faster danced widdershins around him. Overhead, the lightning leaping from bound to bound of the sky held their leaping figures silhouetted for mad fractions of a second in its glare. Thunder drummed through their chanting, and burst with a crash that momentarily drowned the rising frenzy of their voices.

Louder, faster, shriller... The chanting dance was growing to a climax with the climax of the storm. Flashing, crashing... The forces overhead were rending the sky, tearing it open... Adam dug his hands into the sand, dug uselessly, finding no grip that would help him restrain the howl of terrified, animal protest rising in his throat. Teeth fastened on lip he restrained the howl, and bit, not realising he had done so as a shape started up in the lightning's glare; a tall black shape poised at the top of the dunes facing him across the hollow.

Claw-tipped arms flung wide, black dragon-wings flaring, it towered against the brief, lurid backdrop of the lightning.

The dancing witches halted, as abruptly as if struck paralysed. From the wide-open mouth of the apparition came a sound that was half-snarl, half-roar, and with shrieks and moans of reply the witches faced the dunes and grovelled in homage before it.

Dr. Fian was the first to rise to his feet again. A stunned Adam saw him approach the foot of the dune on which the Devil stood, and begin to clamber upwards. Only then did Adam realise that the Devil appeared to have some object gripped in one of his claws, and now he was reaching this object down to Fian's clambering figure.

A mutter of words passed between them as Fian took the object, and the sound drifting across the hollow to Adam aroused his curiosity. With his mind beginning to shake free from the shock of fear it had endured, he strained to make out its meaning, but no sense emerged from the mumble. Fian turned to slither down to the witches again. They rose, making room for him to join their circle, and with another mutter of words he passed the object the Devil had given him to the witch on his right hand.

The witch on Fian's right held it for a moment, then muttering also, she passed it to the neighbour on her right. Again the movement and the sound were repeated, and yet again, and Adam realised that the Devil had intended the object passing from hand to hand to travel anti-clockwise round the entire circle of thirty-nine witches. Eagerly he listened for some hint of the formula that was being recited each time it changed hands, and twice he thought he heard the word "image" emerging from the general muttering. Then quite clearly he heard the name "James", but after that, nothing.

The object reached the woman standing on Fian's left. She dealt with it as all the others had done, but just as Fian was about to receive it back from her, the woman on his right leaned over and snatched it from him. Running to the centre of the circle she held it aloft and yelled,

"Now, now for the burning! Bring fire, sisters and brothers —fire in the Devil's name!"

A massed answering yell came from the witches. They broke from their places to surge around her, but with a howl of rage the Devil leapt down from his high watching-place and charged in among them.

"Fools! Fools! Fools!" Bellowing he snatched the object back, and holding it high out of the witches' reach, raged at them, "Is this one to go to the fire with only a curse and a naming? You crawling, lousy bunglers! Do you not know there is more yet to be done before he dies?"

The witches shrank back from him, but the woman who had snatched the object from Fian stood her ground and called boldly,

"We were promised a death, and a death we will have!"

The towering figure of the Devil froze motionless for an instant, then leapt, with talons striking out to fasten in the witch's hair and drag her to the ground. She went down shrieking, and crouching over her fallen body he snarled,

"Cry mercy, woman, cry mercy, or you will not need to wait until you die to see hell!"

"My lord, my lord..." the woman began whimpering, but Adam did not wait to see what happened to her. Heart knocking with fear, stomach heaving in disgust, he backed away through the rushes and slid rapidly down the further side of the sand-dune. As fast as the shifting sand would allow him to move then, he blundered towards the waste-land, and took to his heels across it.

The rain began as he struck the track on the farther side of the waste-land, heavy, pelting rain that soaked him to the skin long before he had skirted Prestonpans and reached the Birsley track. There was no question of sheltering from the storm now, however. It would not be long, he guessed, before the rain broke up the witches' meeting, and so to linger anywhere in that vicinity would be to risk discovery as they scattered homewards.

Head down against the force of the rain he hurried on up the Birsley track, his only desire to put as much distance as possible between himself and the scenes he had just witnessed; and with huge relief, gained the entrance to Seton's stable-yard at last. His panting breath sounded loud in the arched passageway leading in from the street, and he paused to allow it to quieten before he crossed to the final shelter of the out-house.

Leaning against the passage wall, he watched the rain still striking hard off the cobblestones of the street, and thought of the witches' meeting as he watched. They had gathered in that hollow to murder someone. He was sure of that now, for that was the only explanation which could link the words "image" and "James" with all the references to fire and burning.

They were going to put an image of a man called James in a fire, so that the man himself would die as the image melted. That was another thing he had heard tell witches could do. And Gilly Duncan was part of that Devil's work. Gilly was a murderer too. Yet he had almost been on the point of being sorry for her!

Anger rose in Adam's mind, anger at himself. He was a bigger fool than Gilly, he thought bitterly, for she was weak by nature where he was strong yet still he had been stupid enough to forget the lesson he had learned that day at the gallows' foot. But never again, he vowed. Never again would he yield to the weakness of compassion—more especially compassion for a witch. Let Gilly Duncan appear now and he would tell her so.

He waited for the opportunity, tensing his wet body to keep from shivering as he listened for sounds that would warn of her approach, and anger fed on anger as he waited. His mind overflowed with it. He could feel it smarting in his eyes, burning in his finger-tips, but now it was a totally unreasoning anger rooted in the disgust and fear he had felt at the witches' meeting, and so now it was all directed at Gilly. He would show her, Adam promised himself, not bothering to think what he meant by this. He flexed his fingers at the faint slip-slop of footsteps on the cobbles outside, and sprang as Gilly rounded the corner of the archway.

She gasped as he gripped her, but did not cry out. Her face upturned to his was white in the archway's gloom, her eyes two pools of darkness in the pale blur. Her arms were thin and fragile as sticks under his hands but he tightened his grip cruelly and shook her, whispering roughly,

"I saw you, you witch's spawn! I saw all of you to-night, crawling in front of the Devil. I saw you, d'ye hear? And you will not deceive me again with your timid ways, you—you murderer!"

Gilly gasped again under his shaking; then suddenly she laughed, a weak, sobbing laugh that was more helpless than tears.

"Aye, God forgive us all," she said brokenly through her laughter, "for we have bewitched the King to his death, we—"

As suddenly as it had begun, the foolish laughter stopped. Gilly's head darted downwards, and her teeth bit sharply into Adam's hand. With an exclamation of pain he released her, and swift and silent as a cat she glided off to disappear through the kitchen door.

Chapter 5

THE RED CORD

Like two fencers in a bout where the engagement has begun to seem like real battle, Adam and Master Grahame faced one another. A flush of embarrassment showed through the tan of Adam's skin. Master Grahame was frowning, and anger had raised patches of colour also on the high cheekbones of his face.

"You have lied to me—deceived me!" he accused, and Adam protested,

"Not willingly, sir. And I told no lies."

"Half-truths, lies—'tis all the same. All are dishonest."

"But I had no choice—"

"No choice! Could you not have trusted me?"

"Yes, yes, but I had promised Gilly! I swore I would not betray her for a witch—swore it on the Holy Bible!"

"Yet now you tell me all about this Esbat you witnessed," Grahame exclaimed, "and so you have betrayed her. You followed her there, you said. You saw her dancing and chanting with all the other witches—"

"And so now I am no longer bound by any promise to her," Adam interrupted. "It was murder that raised these antics— remember that, Master Grahame—and I owe no loyalty to a murderer."

"Well..." The patches of angry red faded from Grahame's face as he stood considering this reply, and Adam began to breathe more easily. It had been a most uncomfortable few moments, he thought wryly, but it was still a relief to have spoken freely at last of Gilly and the witches. Now there would be no more awkward questions to parry, no more secrets to hide from Master Grahame. Now, thank goodness, they would be able to get back to the old footing with one another.

"There is some excuse for you, I suppose," Grahame's voice broke into his thoughts. "This Gilly seems to be a pitiable creature, after all, rather than a wicked one, and at least now you have had the sense to be open with me about your discoveries."

"They were not pleasant secrets to have," Adam assured him. "I am glad to have rid my mind of them at last, I can tell you!"

"But that is all that concerns you, eh?"

"Why..." Adam glanced up, surprised at the sudden bitterness in the tone of the question. "Yes, sir," he agreed, but Grahame was not listening for an answer. Eyes brooding on space, he muttered something to himself, then his voice came in a louder mutter,

"But witchcraft against the King—has he gone mad? Or is it some other who—"

Abruptly interrupting himself he began pacing up and down his workshop, frowning, biting his lip to control a sudden shaking of his features; and waiting for him to speak, Adam thought how strangely all this contrasted with his usual calm, and how strangely also it resembled the first occasion they had discussed Gilly and the witches.

Master Grahame, he reflected, had seemed distressed then also—oddly distressed; and he was equally distressed now. But why? Why should he be so concerned to hear about the Esbat when the witches' spell was not aimed at him? Why should it cause *him* distress?

"We have got to do something about this business."

Grahame halted his pacing to make the pronouncement, and Adam stared at him. "Why?" he asked blankly. "The King is none of our affair—none of mine, anyway."

"Do you mean to say you do not care that the King may die?" Grahame took a step towards him, face flushing with anger again, but Adam held his ground and demanded,

"Why should I care? I know nothing of him, except that he lives in a palace in Edinburgh town—and sits on a throne like all other kings, I suppose."

"And is a young man, newly-married, with no child to succeed him," Grahame added forcefully. "Which means there will be civil war in Scotland if he dies—or perhaps an invasion by some foreign power eager to claim the throne. Does that tell you how serious the matter is?"

"I never said it was not serious," Adam defended himself. "I only said it was not my concern."

"It *is* your concern," Grahame insisted, "and mine, and that of every good subject in this land. That is why we must do something about it."

"Then why not go to the King himself and tell him about the Esbat?"

"What?" Grahame glared, as if suspecting a joke at his own expense, but saw nothing except innocence in Adam's face, "It is not so easy as you think to gain audience of the King," he said impatiently, "but even if it was, *my* word would not be acceptable over this. Alchemy is a suspect profession, boy; nearly as suspect as witchcraft! Moreover, there are certain —certain difficulties which make it impossible for me to appear at Court."

"Then send a warning through some other gentleman," Adam suggested, "some friend you can trust to speak for you."

Grahame shook his head. "No, it is too soon for such a move. We have no evidence to support it. A warning now would only succeed in driving the witches underground, leaving them free to try again at some later date. Then we would never discover why they wish to kill the King; and that is important, for once we know the *why* of this matter, we will know whose brain is directing it."

Whose brain... It made no sense, Adam decided, and said protestingly, "But Master Grahame, we know already who orders the witches' doings. 'Tis the Devil who is their master; and how can you discover why the Devil should want to kill the King?"

Grahame ignored him, staring into space again and muttering, "No, my hands are tied in this. There is nothing I can do —for the moment, anyway."

The unfocused gaze came back to rest on Adam. "But *you* can do something. You have a lead to the witches through Gilly Duncan, and you could find out more about their plans from her."

"Oh, no, Master Grahame!" Adam retreated a step, ready to back up his refusal with flight. "I have had enough of witches and their cantrips. I will meddle no more with them."

"Wait, Adam!" Grahame commanded, then quickly changed his tone to a coaxing one. "Just think, Adam. Think for a moment. If the King dies by witchcraft, there will be a most massive hunt for those responsible, and Gilly will be among the witches caught in the drag-net. But if you could persuade her to tell you more of the witches' plan, I would try to find some means to defeat it. And thus Gilly might yet be saved from the justice-fire."

"And why should you think I care whether Gilly burns or not?" Adam demanded. "I have ventured my life sufficiently for her, it seems to me. Why should I risk it again?"

"Because she is so young—younger than you," Grahame told him quietly. "Because she is a witch against her will, and because she is helpless to save herself."

"That is her look-out," Adam retorted. Grahame eyed him in silence for a moment, then quietly again, he asked,

"Do you feel no compassion for her, Adam?"

It was not a fair question, Adam told himself; not fair at all, and answered resentfully, "I have told you before, Master Grahame. There is no room in my life for such weakness."

"Compassion is not a weakness, you fool! It is a strength!" There was an edge of scorn on Grahame's voice now, but it smoothed into gentleness as he added, "God grant you live to learn that, Adam."

Adam was silent, his look defiant, disbelieving. Grahame stared at him, as if staring alone could penetrate to the mind behind that stubborn face, and heard a quick succession of questions in his own mind.

How much more of the truth would it be necessary to tell now? How much could he risk telling without being sure of Adam's help? Should he test to find out what the answer might be?

"Adam..." Hesitantly, Grahame spoke again. "What if ... what if I told you it is *I* who need your compassion?"

"You, sir? But why should—" Adam paused, completing the sentence in his own mind. *Why should a gentleman need compassion from a mere orra-lad?*

The question was a trap, he told himself warily. There was something mysterious about Master Grahame's interest in the witches' activities, something that went beyond his concern with the spell against the King; and this was a trick to draw him into that mystery.

"What would you say to that?" Grahame dropped his question into the silence between them, and without surprise saw Adam's face harden again and heard his sullen answer,

"The same, sir. I have enough to do to take care of myself, and I will peril my soul no longer against witches."

Dark eyes met dark eyes, Grahame's sombre, Adam's uneasy; then quietly Grahame said, "You must learn to trust someone, sometime, or your soul is already lost. Remember that, Adam, and come to me when *you* need help."

"I—" Adam stammered, "I—", then swung round and ran for the door; ran quickly in sudden fear of the impulse urging him to admit that he had changed his mind, that he *did* want to help, *would* venture once more against the witches...

Outside the alchemist's house he paused to gather his scattered wits, then set off homewards at a brisk pace that grew rapidly to a run again. Fast as he ran this time, however, he still could not shake off the sense of reproach that clung to him, and it was only the sight of Jardine in the stable-yard that brought his instinct of self-preservation back into play again. There would be questions asked about his long absence from the yard, he realised, and prepared boldly to divert attention from this.

Jardine was busy watering a fat grey mare that was a stranger to Seton's stable, and pausing by the creature Adam remarked,

"That's a sturdy-looking beast; but a bit over-fed, would you say?"

"Y'are sharp to-day," Jardine approved sourly, and nodded towards the kitchen window. "'Tis hers—the big woman that brought Gilly Duncan to work here; the Wise Wife of Keith, herself."

With a sly, sideways glance that took in Adam's expression without seeming to note it, he added, "Did you know that is what they call her?"

"Mistress Sampson, you mean?" With an effort Adam switched his gaze from the window that showed him Mistress

Sampson seated with Mistress Tait in the kitchen, and tried to speak casually,

"I—someone once pointed her out to me as the woman who brought Gilly here, but I do not know that name for her."

"You should keep your ears open wider," Jardine told him maliciously. "Your eyes too, then maybe you would—"

"Adam!" The kitchen window swung wide as Mistress Tait pushed it to lean out and shout, "Adam! Where the devil have you been, boy? Come here and make yourself useful."

"At once, mistress," Adam called, and would have suited the action to the word if Jardine had not caught his arm and hissed,

"Aye, where *have* you been? 'Tis an hour since I sent you on that errand to the blacksmith!"

"I had to wait the smith's pleasure," Adam lied. "There were others with business before me." And pulling free of Jardine, he ran towards the kitchen.

On the threshold of the open door he paused to hear Mistress Tait's orders, and saw her in the act of resuming her seat at the table with her gaze directed at Mistress Sampson seated opposite her. She looked flustered, but Mistress Sampson sat placidly with not a hair out of place under the starched wings of her cap. Gilly stood between them, pale and nervous-looking as usual, fingers twisted in her apron, her eyes lowered to the level of the red cord looped decoratively across the bodice of Mistress Sampson's gown. Mistress Tait turned briefly to look at him and commanded,

"Look after that spit, Adam, and be sure you will feel my bittling-stick across your back if you let the meat burn."

Involuntarily Adam glanced to the rack holding the heavy, rounded stave that Mistress Tait used for stirring the porridge, then he moved to the roast of meat sputtering over the bed of hot coals in the fireplace. The spit was Gilly's work, he thought as he moved, and Mistress Sampson was evidently the reason why she could not be spared at that moment. Kneeling down to turn the meat slowly on its spit, he listened as Mistress Sampson took up the conversation again.

". . . and as I was saying, mistress, it contents me to hear you are pleased with the girl's work, for I would not wish Master

Seton to regret the hiring-fee he paid for her. But what of her behaviour? Is she honest and obedient?"

"Oh, aye, she is all that," Mistress Tait agreed.

"Good!" With her doll-mouth shaping a tiny smile on her big face, Mistress Sampson nodded and looked up at Gilly. "That pleases me also, girl. Do you hear?"

Whispering, not lifting her eyes from the bright line of red on Mistress Sampson's gown, Gilly answered, "Yes, mistress," and the catechism continued,

"And are you obedient to God also, Gilly?"

"Yes, mistress."

"And say your prayers every night, as you were taught?"

"Yes, mistress."

Adam grasped the handle of the spit so hard at the whispered lies, that the hot metal burned his palm. Exclaiming, he withdrew his hand, and Mistress Tait threw a frowning glance at him before she remarked,

"But the girl is too pale for my taste, Mistress Sampson. It is not a healthy sign, and also she is very nervous."

Her voice rose to a louder, shriller tone, and took on a complaining note that matched her flustered appearance. "Why, 'twas only yesterday she dropped an ashet full of meat when I spoke suddenly to her, and that is not the first dish I have had broken for the same reason. She needs some physic to settle such nervousness, if you ask me, and a good purge to clear the unhealthy vapours from her blood."

"I will make a dose for her to take, and send it to you," Mistress Sampson answered soothingly. "But now, Mistress Tait, could you give us a short time alone together? To pray, you understand, in remembrance of Gilly's poor dead mother. She was my friend, as you know, and 'twas something I promised her before she died."

"Surely," Mistress Tait agreed, but she rose unwillingly all the same, with a doubtful glance at the meat on the spit. "A small prayer?" she suggested. "My meat ... you understand? Master Seton cannot abide a burnt roast."

"A few moments—that is all we need to knock at heaven's door," Mistress Sampson assured her gravely, and with a shrug of acceptance Mistress Tait turned to Adam.

"Out to the pantry," she ordered sourly. "There is a task

there you can do for me while I still have *some* hands to help with the work."

Obediently Adam rose from his knees to follow her as she swept towards the pantry, and glanced at Gilly as he passed by the table. She was still gazing at the twist of red decorating Mistress Sampson's gown, he noted, and wondered at her fixed, unblinking stare. There was something about that stare, something that touched uneasily on a chord of memory... Shifting a meal-tub in the pantry at Mistress Tait's command, Adam let his mind dwell on the memory.

It had been early on a morning that summer, he recalled, and he had come suddenly on the sight of a young rabbit face to face with a weasel. The weasel had been balancing on its hind legs with its forequarters moving in a curious, swaying dance, and the rabbit was crouched low in a trance of terror, with its bulging eyes fixed and staring at the enemy.

That was the kind of trance that seemed to be holding Gilly now; but a shout, and a stamp on the ground had been enough to break the spell on the rabbit before the weasel could leap for its throat, and if—

"Adam! Stir yourself!"

Mistress Tait's scolding voice in his ear brought Adam hurriedly back to the present, and as he renewed his efforts to drag the meal-tub to its new position, she found a different target for her scolding.

"That Sampson woman," she complained, "She says she came here to enquire after Gilly's work, but 'tis my belief she only came to see what she could see in my kitchen. 'Wise Wife', forsooth! If she is wise at all it is only because she is always prying into other folks' affairs, and I have a good mind to tell her so!"

Angrily Mistress Tait threw down the meal measure she had been about to use, and stamped to the pantry door. A second or two later Adam heard her say,

"Ah, so you have finished with Gilly, Mistress Sampson. Well, now, it is my turn to have a private word with you."

"Willingly, Mistress Tait."

The reply in Mistress Sampson's pleasant voice sounded farther away from the pantry door, and as Mistress Tait took up the conversation the sound of her voice diminished also.

Adam risked a look out from the pantry, and saw them walking together to the kitchen door and out into the stable-yard. He looked at Gilly and saw her moving towards the fireplace. Through the window he glimpsed Jardine appearing with Mistress Sampson's grey mare. Gilly dropped to her knees on the hearth, reaching out a listless hand to turn the spit, and Adam moved quickly to stand over her. In a low voice he accused,

"You told a pack of lies just now!"

"My life is all lies," Gilly answered dully, and looked up for a moment with eyes vacant as an idiot's before she went back to her listless turning of the spit.

Adam bit his lip in vexation at her lack of response. If only she would be angry with him, he thought, he would be able to vent the anger he felt against her; but as it was, he could feel the solid core of his own anger crumbling away like sand. Fiercely he tried to recall it, and accused again,

"'Tis all your own fault then. I told you once before you do not need to be a witch against your will, and you did not have to let that Sampson woman bully you into telling lies. Tell the truth and shame the Devil, they say, and that is what you should have done."

Gilly looked up again. The sense had come back into her eyes, and with a shock Adam realised that where she might have wept before, she was now in a state beyond tears. Quietly, and still with that look of terrible calm on her face, she asked,

"Did you see that red cord on Mistress Sampson's gown?"

"Eh?" Puzzled, Adam frowned at her. "What has a red cord to do with telling lies?"

"A great deal," the calm voice assured him. "Mistress Sampson bears the title of 'The Maiden', which means she is official executioner to the witch-covens; and she came here to-day to threaten me with death if I betrayed their secrets. It is that same cord she will use to strangle me when she carries out her office as Maiden."

Gilly paused, while Adam stared appalled at her. He stammered, groping for words to express the tumult of feelings her words had aroused, but Gilly continued over his stammering,

"I have been afraid of this of course, ever since I was elected the thirteenth member of Dr. Fian's coven, for although the

witches respect my power of healing, they still do not trust my
loyalty to their secrets. They have never forgotten, you see,
that I am a witch unwilling; and if the witchcraft they have
in hand just now should fail, they will blame me. Then Agnes
Sampson will strangle me with her red cord—silently,
secretly, so that none but the witches will ever know why I
died, or who killed me."

Slowly Gilly lowered her gaze to the spit again, and for
a long moment the hiss and sputter of hot fat dropping from
the meat to the coals was the only sound in the kitchen.

"Leave me now, Adam," she said eventually. "You have
scolded enough to my discredit, and now I will that you leave
me to find what peace I can before I die."

"But Gilly—" Adam began, and then stood silent, overcome
by the enormity of a new thought opening in his mind. Gilly
did not stir, and he tried again.

"But Gilly, if the witches do succeed in killing the King
by a spell, there will be a most fearsome witch-hunt and you
will be discovered along with all the others. And so—you
must die anyway! If the strangling-cord does not claim you,
the justice-fire will!"

"I know," the small, tired voice from the hearth told him.
"I am marked for death whichever way I turn. There is no
way to escape it."

"But there is—there is!"

With a picture of the alchemist flashing into his mind,
Adam burst out with the words before he realised what he
was saying, then paused, bewildered at himself. The rabbit
and the weasel, he thought; the stamp of the foot! But why
had he stamped his foot then, and shouted? Because he could
not bear to see so helpless a creature die cruelly? And why was
he shouting at Gilly now?

Staring down at her he was shocked again to realise she
was too far gone in despair even to have heard his cry; then
glancing swiftly to the window saw his time run out as Mistress
Tait began turning back towards the kitchen door. His
thoughts raced, frantically seeking a decision.

If only Gilly had made some plea ... If only she had begged
his help, so that he could have argued with her—justified his
refusal, as he had justified it to Master Grahame! But Gilly

was accepting her fate. She was as helpless before it as the
rabbit before the weasel ... the fool, the fool, the poor gentle
fool! ... shout, stamp ... break the spell ... run quick, rabbit,
before the weasel gets you ... run quick from the red cord ...
the murderous hands ... run from the crackle of the justice-
fire ... run, Gilly, run ... !

With a rage of frustration rising in his throat, Adam stared
again at Gilly's bowed head. He was trapped, he thought
wildly; as trapped as she was in her own fate. And in spite of
all his hard words to Master Grahame, it was compassion for
her that had snared him after all!

But he was no helpless victim like her; he knew how to
fight back against the witches, and he *would* fight—for both
of them now! Swiftly he bent to grasp Gilly by the shoulders.
She gasped in the pain of his grip, and with forceful speed he
told her,

"You need not die. I know someone who can prevent it—
a learned man who knows all about witches. I will take you
to him to-night. Leave the kitchen door unlocked and I will
come for you."

There was no time to say more, no time to make sure she
had understood him. With a rush and a bound, Adam re-
gained the pantry and set up a great banging and clattering
to advertise his presence there as Mistress Tait came back into
the kitchen.

Chapter 6

AGAINST THE DARK LEGION

Now there were three of them against the dark legion of the witches! With satisfaction, Adam glanced from the tall figure at the desk to the small one of Gilly following him into Master Grahame's workshop, and thought how easy it had all been this far—much easier than he had expected!

He had not been sure, after all, that Gilly had understood his rapid instructions that afternoon, but even if she had grasped his meaning there had still been the question of whether she would agree to his plan and leave the kitchen door open for him. Yet here they both were now, large as life, and the only uneasy moment had been when they were stealing out of the kitchen together and he had imagined hearing some sound from the stable-hands' bothy. With a smile of encouragement as Gilly returned his glance, he advanced from the doorway and boldly answered the question on Grahame's face.

"I am sorry to disturb you at this time of night, Master Grahame, but you said I should come to you if ever I needed help, and now I am taking you at your word."

"You do not disturb me, Adam; but you surprise me. I admit it; you surprise me." Grahame considered him curiously for a further moment, then his look travelled to Gilly and drily he observed, "And this, I take it, is Gilly Duncan."

"Yes, sir." Adam nodded. "I have told her you can save her from the witches."

"Indeed?" Grahame raised his hand in the familiar rasping gesture across his chin, and lowered his voice to a murmur behind the masking fingers. "What has caused your change of heart, Adam?"

It was not a thing he could possibly explain to anyone,

Adam thought ruefully, and felt himself flushing as he mumbled, "Her life is in double jeopardy, sir, and—"

Frowning, Grahame interrupted, "Double jeopardy?"

"Yes, sir. The witches suspect her of betraying their plan to kill the King and if it fails, she will be strangled by a woman called Agnes Sampson."

"*The Maiden!*" Grahame breathed. "I see! Now I see, Adam. 'Tis death by the red cord for her on the one hand, or death by the justice-fire on the other. And you—?"

"I—I found I was sorry for her after all."

Grahame smiled at the reluctant admission, a slow friendly smile that wiped out any trace of the quarrel between them, then looked beyond him to Gilly again. She was still standing out of earshot of their quiet conversation, her head turning occasionally for a nervous glance into the shadows of the candle-lit workshop. He beckoned her. She came hesitantly forward, and with quickening interest he recalled Adam's mention of her healing powers.

It was more than possible of course, he mused, that she could have such a gift; nor was it something that needed any aid of witchcraft. From time out of mind, after all, there had been learned men who argued for the existence of a universal life-force which could be directed towards healing; and their learning had constantly been applied in attempts to tap its source. Yet ironically, it was often through simple peasants such as this Gilly that the healing life-force chose to channel itself!

She had ducked him a little curtsy now and was standing beside Adam, her fair head level with his shoulder and face pearl-pale in the soft candle-light. Her eyes were blue, Grahame noted. They looked large in her thin face and they had a strangely luminous quality... *Power over animals*... That was another gift Adam had ascribed to her, and he could well believe there was some such mystery behind that haunting glance.

"Adam has told me a little about you, Gilly," he said gently, "and now I need to know more. Yet you say nothing, and I think this is because you are not sure you can trust me with this information."

"That is true, sir," Gilly answered him gravely, "and I

cannot even think about trusting you until—"

"Until you have proof that I am able to defeat the witches," Grahame took the words away from her. "Well, that is a fair enough demand." He pondered it, rasping away at his chin, then faintly smiling he asked,

"Are you frightened of the Devil and his fiery horse, Gilly?"

She nodded, and Grahame's smile widened. "I can banish that fear for you, here and now," he remarked, and moved briskly to the shelves that held his jars of chemicals. Choosing two from among them, he carried them over to his workbench, then drew an earthenware bowl and a pair of forceps towards him.

"Come here," he told Adam and Gilly, and as they obeyed him he moved about snuffing out all the candles except the one that lit the work-bench itself. Deftly then he removed the lid of one jar and tipped it up over the bowl. The contents poured out, filling the bowl with liquid that gleamed deep gold in the candle's paler flame, and watching it pour he explained,

"This, my children, is oil of olives, made by pressing the fruit of the olive tree."

The bowl full, he set the first jar down and opened the second one. Forceps in hand, he dipped inside this second jar, and withdrew the forceps holding a small lump of an almost transparent wax-like substance that dripped water from the jar on to the bench. A quick movement transferred the waxy substance to the bowl, and as the forceps released it to settle into the oil Grahame continued,

"And that stuff which looks like wax is a mineral named white phosphorus, here seen in the pure form which—among other methods—can be obtained by treating the ash of roasted bones in certain ways. Normally, as you have seen, pure phosphorus is kept in water, which cannot dissolve it, yet excludes all other contact with it. But now—"

The gleaming gold of the oil had begun to cloud slightly as he spoke, and reaching out to extinguish the one remaining candle he finished,

"Now watch!"

The smoke of the candle hung on the darkened air of the workshop, and in the depth of the bowl something glimmered.

The after-image of the candle's light, Adam thought, then saw the glimmer grow slowly to a blue glow that spread and strengthened, and further spread until it filled the whole extent of the bowl with cold blue light. Pale fingers appeared beside the bowl as Grahame put forth a hand to rock it gently. The cold blue glow danced eerily in the darkness with the movement of the bowl, and a faint acrid smell arose from it. Adam sniffed, then coughed as the acrid taint caught at his throat, and with a pang of remembered fear shooting through him heard Grahame ask,

"You recognise the light, eh, Adam? And the smell?"

"They are the same, the very same as I met with on Lammas Eve," Adam managed through his coughing, and backed uneasily from the work-bench. Gilly blundered against him, exclaiming as she too retreated in fear of the strange blue glow, and quickly Grahame tried to re-assure them,

"There is no need to be afraid. 'Tis the natural property of phosphorus to burn under certain conditions, and one such condition occurs when it is dissolved in oil of olives. That is the sole cause of the blue glow you see now."

There was a scratching sound as he struck flint to make a spark, and a second later he was touching the candle-wick to glowing tinder. A welcome yellow flame sprang up, and as he moved around lighting other candles from it, Adam and Gilly looked a mutual question at one another. Grahame came towards them and replaced the work-bench candle in its holder.

"So!" Picking up a flat dish from the bench he covered the bowl's contents with it then stepped back, smiling. "Now you have learned the secret of the Devil's fiery horse!"

"Phosphorus....!" Muttering, Adam tried out the strange word, and stared doubtfully at the covered bowl.

Gilly looked bewildered, and patiently Grahame enlarged his explanation for her. "The Devil's horse is no supernatural creature as you have always supposed, Gilly, but simply an ordinary horse with a solution of phosphorus in oil of olives smeared over its body to make it glow blue in the darkness."

"But surely," Adam objected, "when this—this phosphorus burned as we have just seen it doing, it would injure the hide of the horse."

"Possibly," Grahame acknowledged, "but not until all the oil had evaporated, which would be a slow process. Moreover, it would be simple to protect the creature's hide by painting the solution on to some covering laid over it. 'Tis a common enough trick."

Incredulously Adam repeated, "A common trick?"

Grahame shrugged. "There are many alchemists who are more rogues than true philosophers; and when such a one enters into unholy alliance with a sorcerer or his like, this is one of the methods used to counterfeit the appearance of some ghostly creature."

"'Twas a terrible unkindness to the horse, all the same," Gilly said unexpectedly. She looked indignant now, her bewilderment gone and her uneasiness with Grahame apparently vanquished by concern for the horse. "It must have suffered fear of the blue fire even though it was not in pain," she added, and Adam was taken aback to realise that her indignation meant she had accepted Grahame's theory.

"But Gilly," he exclaimed, "the Devil has all Hell at his command, surely? Why should he need to use an ordinary horse and play such a trick with it when he could summon any monster he chooses to ride?"

Gilly stared at him, the significance of his words slowly sinking home, then as one person they turned to look at Grahame. Gravely he met their looks, and slowly, making each word tell, he answered Adam's questions.

"Because the creature you take to be the Devil is not a supernatural being either. He is a man, like any other man."

In the stunned silence that followed, Grahame studied the emotions apparent on each face. Thirty years of self-discipline kept his own face impassive, but still he could not prevent the sweat starting out on his brow, nor could he escape the anguish that gripped him as he tried to assess the impact of his words. The old tormenting fear once again found voice in him.

How much more—oh, dear God, how much more of the truth would he have to reveal now to convince these children! The boy was amenable to reason. Sensible argument, some logical proof that stopped just short of the final revelation might be enough to engage his belief. But the girl—this girl with the gentle mystic's face and the haunting eyes; he would have to rely on the force of persuasion alone to combat her superstitious dread. She would have to be moved somehow to trust him—trust him as absolutely as if he were God Almighty himself come to fight the Devil on her behalf...

Raising a hand to dab at his sweating brow he became aware of Adam protesting, "But his face, Master Grahame! It was a beast-face, with horns sprouting from the head. And he had claws instead of hands—I saw them!"

"No," Grahame told him quietly. "That was another deception. What you saw was a man dressed in the mask and skin of an animal; a man disguised as a beast."

Adam gaped for a moment then swung round to demand of Gilly, "Is that true? You must have seen him close, Gilly. Is he truly a man like other men?"

Grahame added, "You have even touched him, Gilly, as all witches must touch the Devil when they do homage to him. Tell Adam how that touch felt."

"It was cold," Gilly said faintly, "cold and—and dead. And hard. And he stank, like an animal."

"Or like a man wearing the hide of an animal," Grahame suggested, "a badly-flayed hide grown hard and stinking with the passage of time."

"But *what* man?" With a gesture of frustration, Adam turned away from Gilly. "Who is he, Master Grahame?"

"Wait, and you will learn," Grahame told him. "And remember, I have never lied to you. Gilly—"

"Yes, sir!" Obediently Gilly gave him her attention, and he asked,

"The covens have a Grand Master, have they not, Gilly? And when two or more covens attend an Esbat together, it is the Grand Master who presides over their meeting?"

Gilly nodded yes to each question, and he pursued, "But when Grand Sabbat is held, it is the Devil who presides over it, and there is no sign of the Grand Master then—is there, Gilly? In fact, there has never been a witch-meeting when both the Grand Master and the Devil were present together. Is that not so?"

Once again Gilly nodded, her eyes round with wonder now

at the extent of his knowledge, and was even more surprised when he asked,

"What is your Grand Master like, Gilly?"

"I—I have never seen his face," she admitted uncertainly. "He always comes masked to our meetings—but I can tell you that he is a tall man, as tall as you are, sir. And lean-built also, like you."

"Or like the Devil?" Grahame suggested, and cut triumphantly across her mutter of agreement, "There is your answer, Adam! This Grand Master who hides his face and has the same build as the Devil; he is never seen at any meeting where the Devil presides for the simple reason that they are *one and the same person*!"

Adam looked from the urgent pressure of his gaze to the uncertainty on Gilly's face. "That sounds logical enough," he admitted cautiously, "but I think I could find flaws in your argument if I had time to study it."

"Then study it!" With a swift gesture Grahame swept a bundle of papers off his desk and thrust them into Adam's hands. "Study these accounts of witch-trials from all over Europe—from England, France, Germany, Sweden; and in our own country, too, from the towns of Forres, Nairn, Paisley, Pittenweem, and many, many more. The organisation of the witch-covens is the same in all these places. I have been collecting evidence of it for years, and everywhere I find the same pattern of a Grand Master who presides over the covens yet is never present when some so-called 'Devil' *who resembles him in build* appears to the witches. Read, Adam, and ask yourself why this should be!"

Adam looked down at the topmost paper and words leaped out from it to meet his eye ... *our Grand Master comes masked to the meeting* ... *We did homage to the Devil at* ... *like a beast in the shape of a man* ... *and did feel his touch to be cold.* ...

Fascinated, he began reading methodically, and Grahame turned to Gilly. She had drawn apart from their argument, huddling forlornly into herself, and there was a loneliness about the small, withdrawn figure that touched a nerve of pity in him. His voice gentle, he said,

"But this mountebank Devil has deceived you more than

any of the others, has he not, Gilly? For you were only a child when you made your first homage to him—a child who could not be expected to ask questions or to go against her elders. And so you have had years of terror you need never have endured; years of misery believing your soul stolen from you and damned through all eternity. Poor child! Poor gentle, foolish child!"

"No—no, you are wrong! He *is* the Devil, Master Grahame." In faint, breathless tones, Gilly protested against the persuasion in his voice. "He can do such things—appearing from nowhere, disappearing again in a cloud of smoke—such things as only the Devil could do."

"Trickery—all trickery," Grahame told her. "I could show you twenty such tricks in as many minutes with my chemicals, Gilly. Any hedgerow gipsy or juggler would show you as many more counterfeit wonders for the price of a loaf. But you take his tricks for real magic because you are afraid of him, and fear is always blind."

"But—but he is evil," Gilly stammered. "He preaches wrong-doing to us at the Sabbats, asking what wickedness we have done since we last saw him. No man could be so evil."

"What can you know of man's evil!" Grahame exclaimed. "You are only a child, and the souls of all children remain very close to God. Yours has much further to wander from Him before you learn how truly evil men can be."

"I have wandered to the lip of Hell already," Gilly answered miserably, but a desire to believe Grahame looked out of her eyes now and she did not shrink when he came close to her and cupped her head between his palms.

"Poor child ... poor lost child ..." Lightly he smoothed the soft hair on the crown of her head, and murmured again; comfortingly, soothingly, like a father ...

Like the father she could only dimly remember, the father who hated witchcraft; who would have scorned her for a witch, too, if she had turned to him. The father whose help she had so often longed to seek ... Gilly's thoughts whirled in a confusion of yearning, and faintly again she protested,

• "There is the stamp of Hell on him, Master Grahame." But the longing to believe now made a question of her words and her eyes beseeched Grahame to tell her she was wrong.

"So there is on all men who abandon God," he told her softly, "and some, like this man, carry it more clearly than others. Yet I can save you from him, Gilly, I can save you from the witches, from death, and from Hell, if only—"

The gentle hands still comforted her head, the dark, deep-set eyes still held her own gaze fixed, but the persuasive voice hesitated and desperately she prompted,

"If only—"

"Trust me," Grahame whispered. "Take your first step in faith, Gilly, and believe he is only a man like other men. Say it! Say it, Gilly, and believe it. *He is only a man like other men.*"

She was drowning ... drowning in waves of fear and doubt; but there were hands holding her head above the waves— warm hands, strong, fatherly hands. There was a rescuer looking down at her. If she could only reach him, hold on to him, she would not die ...

With a quick, convulsive gesture Gilly reached up to clutch at Grahame's wrists, and with a grip of desperation holding on to them, said in a breaking voice,

"He is only a man like other men!"

"Calm, now, calm!" Grahame held her as her grip broke suddenly and she sagged against him. He gave her time to recover herself, aware suddenly of Adam looking up from the bundle of papers with a question blazing in his face. The last question, Grahame realised, avoiding the look; the Grand Master's name—the name of the Devil on the fiery horse.

Gilly's quivering had lessened. He could feel her taut muscles relaxing under his hands, and now she was raising her head to look at him again. Exhaustion was written on her face, in the droop of her mouth and the delicate shadows under her eyes. Like a nurse coaxing he led her to the chair by his desk, and seated her there. She leaned back, her eyes closed, and he told her,

"Adam has already described the Esbat at Aitchison's Haven to me, Gilly, but I need to know more about it than he was able to discover. And I must know everything there is to tell about the plot of the wax image."

Gilly nodded. "Dr. Fian sent us word to meet with the Grand Master," she began, "three covens of us."

As if she had sensed Grahame's frown of question at this, her eyes flew open and she explained, "Dr. Fian is Registrar to the Devil, and summons all our meetings. Also, he has a great black book where he writes all the work the witches do."

"I see." Grahame nodded approval of this attention to detail, and Gilly continued,

"The Grand Master told us that the King's death would be required by means of a wax image that would be roasted in the fire, and Mistress Agnes Sampson, who is the Maiden of the covens, said that she would make the image. But all this put us in great dismay, because twice before we have tried to kill the King—once by casting cats into the sea to raise a storm that would wreck the ship he sailed in, and the other time by means of poison made from the venom of a toad mixed with adder's skin and other foul ingredients. Yet each time we have failed, because there was dispute and jealousy among the leaders of these attempts."

A sharp indrawn breath from Grahame made her pause, and abruptly he demanded,

"But why, Gilly? Why all this murderous intent towards the King?"

"We asked that of the Grand Master too," she told him, "and he said that it is so that another might rule in the King's place—one who is a friend to witches. And he said also that this time we should succeed because we should have the help of the Devil to enchant the image. And Mistress Sampson laughed at this, telling us she would make the image into a good likeness of the King, which was not pleasant to hear. Then the Grand Master instructed her how to prepare the image, which he said must be done in this wise.

"While the wax was still soft, he told her, she must poke the heart of a freshly-killed swallow into it, below the right arm of the image, and the liver of the same bird into the corresponding place on the left side. Round the ribs of the image then, she must bind a paper with these words written on it—*Ailif, casyl, izaze, hit mel meltal*. And the thread used to bind the paper should be new thread, spun from the fleece of a black ewe that had never cast a lamb."

Adam had looked up from the papers in his hand to listen to all this, and the thought of the Sampson woman bent over

her gruesome work made him grimace with distaste. Gilly
was too intent on finishing her tale to notice him, however,
and without a pause she went on,

"When all this had been said, Dr. Fian instructed Mistress
Sampson to bring him the image to be delivered to the Grand
Master, and he also told us that he would raise the Devil for
us at our Esbat at Aitchison's Haven. And this he did, when
we were met together in that place on the night of the great
storm."

"By which time the image had passed to the Devil's
keeping," Grahame added, and asked grimly, "Did you not
wonder how that came about, Gilly?"

"Aye, sir," she admitted, then offered trustingly, "but I do
not wonder at it now that I know the Grand Master and the
Devil are one and the same person."

"Exactly!" With a tight little smile of triumph on his face,
Grahame glanced at Adam and challenged, "You see how
Gilly's story is adding to the proof I have already given you?"

"I do, sir," Adam acknowledged, and held up the bundle of
papers before he returned it to Grahame's desk. "But you have
already convinced me with these."

"And so now all three of us know it is a human agency we
are fighting," Grahame commented briskly. "That is real progress, my children!" He nodded to Gilly, and she continued,

"When we met for our Esbat at Aitchison's Haven, the
Devil gave Dr. Fian the image and told him he must pass it
to each of us in turn. And he said that as each one passed it
to her neighbour, she must put this curse on it: *This is the
image of King James the Sixth, ordered to be consumed at the
instance of a nobleman, Francis, Earl of Bothwell.*"

"Bothwell!" Grahame repeated, and drew a long, sighing
breath of satisfaction. "Now we have arrived at the heart of
the matter!" He glanced at each of them in turn. "Do you
know who this Bothwell is, Gilly? Or you, Adam?"

They shook their heads, looking blankly at him, and grimly
he told them, "Listen then, and you shall hear the real motive
behind the actions of this evil mountebank who poses as the
Devil. Francis Stewart, fifth Earl of Bothwell, is the King's
cousin; and if the King should die now, childless, Bothwell
would have a good claim to succeed him. Think of the

rewards 'the Devil' could hope to receive then, for his help!
And if Bothwell refused such rewards, think of the force of
blackmail this Devil could exert to make him pay up, and
keep silent about paying. And think also of the freedom of
action the witches would have then, under the powerful protection of one who had such a hold over the throne itself. Oh,
'tis a monstrous cunning Devil we have here! But he will not
succeed—I shall not let him succeed!"

Grahame struck a clenched fist into the palm of his other
hand, and glared down at Gilly. "I shall expose this plot," he
told her fiercely, "and you are the evidence I need. You must
come with me to Court, Gilly, and tell the King what you
have just told me."

"And be burned for a witch!" Gilly flinched back from
him, then sprang to her feet, sending her chair crashing to the
ground with the violence of the movement.

"But you said you would save me!" Her voice a whispering
scream, she accused, "You said you would save me—you
promised!"

"Yes..." Grahame stared at her, a dazed look beginning
to replace the excitement in his face. "Yes... I—forgive me,
Gilly. I let myself be carried away. 'Tis not possible to use
you as a witness, of course—or for me to appear at Court. I
had forgotten that. I must think of something else—some
other way. But time—time is important. When is the image
to be burnt, Gilly? How much time have we left?"

Gilly hesitated, looking warily at him, and with sudden
anguish of appeal he begged, "Try to understand, child. I
spoke without thinking, and I—" His voice broke, and in shaking tones he finished, "If the witches succeed in killing the
King, then I must die too, for I cannot live any longer with—
with a certain secret that will have a bearing on that crime."

In silence, puzzled at first and then with pity, Gilly stared
at his haggard face; and quietly into the silence Adam said,

"You know who the Devil is. You have known it all along,
right from the moment I told you about seeing him ride down
Birsley."

Grahame bowed his head, silently acknowledging the truth
of the assertion. Adam was about to speak again, but Gilly

checked him with a gesture; then still with the look of pity for Grahame on her face, she said,

"The next Grand Sabbat will be held on Hallowe'en, in Saint Andrew's Church, hard by the town of North Berwick, and the image will be burned then. The Devil promised us this before we left the Esbat at Aitchison's Haven."

Slowly Grahame raised his head, returning hope wiping some of the lines from his face. "Then there is plenty of time left. Thank God for that, Gilly, thank God!" Relief filled his voice, and he smiled at her. "Forgive me," he begged again. "I have all my senses about me now, and now I know what must be done. The image must be destroyed before it can be put to use. More than that, the Devil's power over the witches must be broken so that he will not be able to persuade them to yet another attempt on the King's life. And you must be removed far from reach of the witches' vengeance."

"Have you thought of a plan already that will accomplish all this?" Adam asked curiously.

"In broad outline, yes," Grahame admitted. "But I must have time to think of the details before I tell you of it— although I can say now that it is something requiring help from both of you. And I shall need some further information from Gilly, if she is still prepared to trust me."

Gilly regarded him gravely. "I trust you," she said. "I will be ready to answer your questions, when you are ready to ask them."

Master Grahame held out a hand to her. She took it without hesitation, re-establishing in a moment, it seemed to Adam, the bond that had existed between them. There was no need for either of them to say more, he realised, and followed quietly as Gilly moved away towards the door. Pausing there while Gilly turned to drop a curtsy of farewell to Grahame, he glanced back with his own gesture of farewell.

Grahame was watching them, his long face inscrutable as ever now, and with a sudden flash of insight Adam realised how skilfully he had managed the interview to suit himself, extracting trust yet giving none in return. On impulse, he aimed at the only chink in the guarded front Grahame had presented, and said bluntly,

"There is one thing you have still not told us about the Devil, Master Grahame—his name!"

Not a muscle stirred in Grahame's face at the challenge, and quietly he answered it, "You must let me keep that secret, Adam, until Hallowe'en at least. Then you will see his face, and there will be no further need to hide his name from you."

His name, his cursed name! And his face—that face of pain, of exile, of unhappy memories; the face of his enemy—his bitter enemy! Sitting at his desk long after Adam and Gilly had left his workshop, Grahame heard the words hammering in his mind. And later still, as he lay sleepless in his four-poster bed, the face that had haunted his exile hovered against the darkness enclosed by the bed-curtains, taunting him, mocking his sleeplessness...

... *the face of his enemy, his bitter, his beloved enemy ...!*

Chapter 7

THE ROAD TO NORTH BERWICK

Adam reached up both hands to cram his bonnet closer down on his head, and wished himself anywhere except crouched on watch at the peak of a wind-swept hill. He peered through the darkness to where the waters of the Firth of Forth showed as a greyish blur a mile northwards of his perch on North Berwick Law, and imagined he could see the little township of North Berwick itself huddled against the coast-line.

But it was only imagination of course, he admitted to himself. On any other night of the year there might have been lights in the town to guide his eye. But not on this night—not on Hallowe'en, when the power of the witches was at its height! There would be no good Christian abroad in North Berwick this night, not one candle burning late, not one door left unlocked in defiance of the dark legion.

Regretfully he pictured his own uncomfortable but safe refuge in Seton's outhouse, and glanced at Gilly crouching beside him. She sat huddled into her cloak, motionless except for a slow turning of her head to scan the dark countryside below the slopes of the Law, and wondering at her apparent calm he called her softly. She turned to look at him, and whispering still he asked,

"Are you not afraid?"

She shook her head, asking softly in her turn, "Are you?"

"I am, when I think of what we have to do," Adam admitted, and felt sudden appalled wonder at having allowed himself to be persuaded into such a situation.

Gilly said, almost reprovingly, "'Tis quite safe, Adam. Master Grahame said so."

And that of course, he told himself, was the secret of her

calm—*Master Grahame said so.* She had trusted him utterly at that first meeting in his work-shop, and his word had continued to be law to her in all the weeks since then. Holy Writ in fact, Adam cynically amended his thought, then was ashamed of the blasphemy even while he envied Gilly's acceptance of the danger they were courting.

Turning to look southwards he studied the stretch of countryside between the Law and the village of Whitekirk, three miles inland from North Berwick. There was one sure way the Devil could take to the Sabbat from Whitekirk—if he came from Whitekirk. But he might equally well come from Prestonpans, of course, or from Longniddry—or even from Tranent, along the way they themselves had just ridden.

Adam glanced down the hill to where Master Grahame waited patiently with the horses he had provided for their night's journeying. The steep rise of the Law commanded a view of every approach to North Berwick, and once they had sighted the blue light of the Devil's horse from their look-out they would be able to place the direction from which it was travelling. It would take only minutes then, to scramble down to rendezvous with Grahame.

That was the first step in the plan he had proposed, and it seemed simple enough now that it had been decided upon; but the deciding had not been a simple matter or a safe one! Uneasily, Adam remembered Jardine.

Those ferrety eyes were still watching him, waiting for him to blunder into something that would mean another beating. And somehow he was sure now that they were watching Gilly also—which was only to be expected, of course, since she had been the cause of Jardine's humiliation in the first place. But there had also been Dod Carnegie to consider in these past few weeks, for Dod was always trying to curry favour with Jardine and could be counted on to report the least thing that looked suspicious. And finally there was Mistress Tait, who had credited Mistress Sampson's physic with Gilly's new-found calm, but who would still have scented something in the wind if she had seen him and Gilly with their heads together in conversation.

"'Tis getting near the time." Gilly spoke quietly, her eyes never ceasing to scan the open countryside spread out all around the hill. "They will be closing in from every side now, Adam."

Adam nodded, feeling his mouth suddenly too dry for speech. The darkness below them hid villages, hamlets, farms, all connected to a pattern of earthen roads, with bridle-tracks leading like tendrils off a main stem to the occasional cottages standing solitary from their neighbours. And now, as Gilly had reminded him, all the figures that had been stealing secretly on foot or riding horses with muffled hooves through this dark network of paths would be converging silently on North Berwick, furtive as wood-lice scurrying from the interstices of rotten timber, and as loathsome! Adam shivered at the thought, and sensing his tremor but mistaking the reason for it, Gilly said,

"Master Grahame's plan will not fail, Adam. And besides, you have covered our tracks too well for anyone to guess at it."

That last part was true at least, Adam thought, and was thankful he had hit on the idea of using Master Seton's dove-cote to avoid the danger of further joint excursions to Master Grahame's work-shop. He himself had plenty of excuse for spending time at the dove-cote, after all, since it was his duty to look after the five hundred nesting-holes that lined the tower. And since pigeon was a main source of fresh meat for Master Seton's table at that time of year and it was Gilly's duty to keep the larder stocked, no-one could possibly have suspected her frequent trips to the dove-cote.

Five hundred pair of pigeon, moreover, made a deal of noise among them! There had been no danger of their conversations being overheard through all the whirr of wings, and cooing, and it had been a simple matter to relay all Gilly's information about the Sabbat in the course of his normal visits to Master Grahame.

And so the plan conceived in outline at that first meeting in the alchemist's work-shop had grown gradually to its final state, with all the details filled in and all the necessary precautions taken, but—

Adam fingered the black face-mask hung around his neck. It was essential for Gilly to attend this Hallowe'en Sabbat, of course, otherwise the witches would immediately assume her suspected betrayal had become a reality. And just in case the plan went awry, it was essential also that he be there to help her escape. The mask was the only answer to that, for Gilly had assured him that most of the witches came masked to the Grand Sabbat for fear of informers in their midst, and with his face thus hidden he would be able to pass undetected among them. But supposing he blundered somehow? Supposing he betrayed himself with some mistaken word, some gesture out of place?

Rapidly Adam reviewed all that Gilly had told him about the ritual of the Sabbat, and to his horror, found a blank spot in his memory. He nudged Gilly and whispered,

"The witch-song, Gilly—the one they sing when they dance the ring-dance; I have forgot the words of it!"

"Listen, 'tis simple: *Commer goe ye before, Commer goe ye; Gif ye will not goe before, Commer let me.*" Gilly waited while he repeated the words, then added, "Remember too, when you join in the ring-dance you must put your hands on the waist of the one in front and not let go, leap he never so wildly. And whatever you do, do not forget to raise that face-mask before we arrive at the Sabbat."

"I do not like the feel of it," Adam grumbled, and perversely felt drawn to experiment with wearing it. The soft black cloth pressed against his face with the smothering feel of a hand in a nightmare. He tugged it away again, his skin prickling with irritation and dislike, and his gaze sweeping inland caught a glow of blue on the horizon.

"There!" One hand shooting out to point, he grasped Gilly's arm with the other. "Do you see it? 'Tis coming from the direction of Whitekirk!"

Gilly gasped. Unsteadily she said, "There is a strong witch-coven in that village, and—"

"And very likely someone there had a horse waiting for him to dress out with his phosphorus trickery," Adam finished for her. "Hurry, Gilly! We must reach Master Grahame now."

Jerking her to her feet with the words, he seized her hand and plunged forward. Gilly already had her skirts kirtled above her knees in preparation for the run downhill to their rendezvous with Grahame, and she tried gamely to keep the reckless pace he set, clinging tightly to his handhold and uttering no protest at being dragged on by his longer stride.

They fell once, missing the path and tripping over an unexpected outcrop of stones. Adam's shirt was hooked by a branch of gorse and almost ripped from his back. Gilly's hair-ribbon was torn off by the same branch, and she ran on blindly behind the thick curtain of hair swinging over her eyes.

They reached the rendezvous too breathless for speech, to find Grahame warned by the sound of their coming and already mounted. Adam vaulted for the saddle of the mount he was sharing with Gilly, gasping out the single word *"Whitekirk!"* as he gathered its reins in one hand and reached out the other to swing Gilly up astride its crupper. Grahame kicked heels to his horse's flanks. Adam followed suit, and as the beasts bounded forward Grahame called,

"Swing to the right at the end of this path. Dismount when I do, tie off your end of the rope at the left side of the road, and hide close beside it. And when I shout for you—jump!"

There was no time to feel fear now! They reached the path's junction with the Whitekirk road before Adam realised it was on them, and with a jerk of the reins he brought his beast's head round to follow Grahame's sudden turn to the right. Another half-mile flew past under them. Trees loomed up ahead on either side of the road and Grahame pulled abruptly to a halt in their shadow. He slid to the ground, a coil of thin black rope held ready over his arm, and tossed one end of it to Adam. Gilly gathered the horses' reins, and as she ran the beasts into the wood on the left side of the road, Adam and Grahame paid out the rope across its breadth.

"Tie off at four feet from the ground and keep it taut," Grahame ordered, and disappeared into the wood with his own end of the rope. Adam crashed up the stony bank on the opposite side of the road, slithered into the ditch beyond it, and scrambled up to pull the rope level and taut before he knotted it firmly round the trunk of a young birch tree. Gilly stood quietly by, holding the horses and murmuring softly to them. Adam took the reins from her and hobbled both animals so that they could not bolt if they panicked at the crucial moment.

"Make sure you keep them quiet," he ordered Gilly, then

made for the bank again and flung himself down against it.
Peering out over the top of the bank he saw the tall dark
shape that was Grahame on the far side of the road, and called
softly,

"All ready, sir."

Grahame called back an acknowledgment and vanished into
the wood again. The sound of his progress ceased, and other
small sounds crept into the silence that followed—a rustle of
autumn foliage, a small creak of harness, the sighing of the
horses' breath. Adam's hands closed tightly over the loose
stones that littered the bank.

Now there was time to feel fear—too much time! Adam
felt his heart-beat stumble and flutter. A vein in his forehead
began to throb. In his mind grew a slow realisation that he
would never be able to play the role Grahame's plan had
assigned him—not even to save his own life, far less the life of
Gilly. But he could back out of the plan altogether! There
were two horses available. He could jump up, seize one of
them, and within seconds be well out of reach of the whole
mad enterprise.

He visualised the sequence of necessary actions, but a
curious inertia seemed to have taken possession of his limbs
and his thoughts had a dream-like quality that told him he
would never translate them to action. He became aware of
Gilly coming to crouch beside him against the bank. She was
shivering, and after a moment she whispered,

"Adam ..." There was a long pause, then the whispering
voice ran rapidly on, "Oh, Adam, I am feared! I am awful
feared he truly is the Devil, Adam. I cannot do as Master
Grahame said. I cannot do it!"

"Nor can I." It was an effort to find enough voice even to
whisper the reply, and in the silence that hung between them
after that, Adam touched a depth of wretchedness and shame
that filled him with sick disgust at himself.

Yet the fault was not his own, he argued, feebly trying to
find a case for himself. It was Master Grahame who should be
blamed—Master Grahame who had used his damnable logic
to convince him that the Devil was only a man in disguise,
yet had failed to realise that a life-time's fear of the Devil was

bound to defeat logic in the end. And trust, too! Gilly was shivering uncontrollably now.

A sudden fierce dislike of seeing his own wretched condition thus reflected in another made Adam edge away from Gilly. The movement brought his attention back to the road, and with a feeling of sickness rising in his throat he saw the blue glow beyond the trees.

Time, space, and distance, all ceased to exist for Adam in that moment. The dark October night, the trees, the road, all receded from his consciousness, and he existed somewhere in an eternity that held only a blue glow bearing down on him out of a great void, growing, growing in size, and changing, changing in shape until his whole vision was filled by the towering spectacle of the fiery horse with the Devil astride it.

The spell broke with the sudden impact of the horse's chest against the unexpected obstacle of the rope. Thrown back on its haunches, the creature pawed the air and wildly snorted its alarm while the rider toppled backwards, the reins flying from his grip and only his feet in the stirrups keeping him from falling clear out of the saddle.

"Adam!" A voice roared in the same moment, and Master Grahame came leaping out of the darkness on the far side of the road to reach up and grapple with the rider. The horse veered round, struggling to regain its balance. The grip Grahame had achieved on the rider wrenched him from the saddle, and they crashed together to the ground.

Yet still Adam did not jump to help him as they had planned, nor did Gilly rush to play her part by seizing the horse's reins and calming it with her hold; still their human flesh shrank in fear of the beast-presence straight from Hell itself, although in Gilly at least, another emotion was beginning to struggle with fear.

The horse had plunged as its rider was dragged clear, then reared in further panic. Now, as it stamped aimless and terrified in the roadway, she rose to her knees muttering,

"Oh, the poor creature—'tis wicked suffering to put on it!"

Biting her thumb in indecision, she hovered at the crest of the bank, then suddenly she was gone, jumping down the bank to the roadway before Adam could fully grasp her intention. She circled the horse, hand and voice coaxing it, then made a sudden snatch at its reins.

"*Adam!* Adam, where are you!" Master Grahame's voice came in an urgent shout from the tangle of legs and arms in the roadway as Gilly seized the horse's bridle in one hand and brought its nose down to be caressed by the other.

"Adam . . . !" Grahame's voice was weaker now, but the paralysis of fear that gripped Adam did not loose its hold. Teeth clenched, hands gripping the stones on a level with his staring eyes, he lay rigid at the top of the bank. And Grahame was underneath the Devil now, his throat held by one clawed hand. The Devil's other arm flew upwards, and a knife glittered briefly in the blue light shed by the horse.

But the Devil would not need a knife to kill! *This was a man!*

Like a revelation it burst on Adam, shocking him back to life, and with a stone clenched in either hand he bounded into the roadway.

Blood showed on Grahame's throat where the Devil's claws had scored it, and he was exerting the last of his strength to hold off the knife arm posed above him. Adam took aim at the great horned head poised above its victim, and howling in mingled hate and fear crashed the stone in his right hand squarely down between the horns. The Devil crumpled slowly forward. Grahame heaved at the sagging body, and it fell away from him. He said thickly,

"You have killed him. Bring the horse nearer. I must have light."

His voice reached Gilly and she began coaxing the horse forward as he knelt beside the body. The creature had calmed under her gentling, but it was still nervous. Stamping, tossing its head, it edged unwillingly near, and Adam saw how it had been protected from the burning action of the phosphorus by painting the oily solution on to coverings that fitted its head, body, and hooves. He glanced back at Grahame in its light, and saw that he had raised the Devil's body to strip it of its disguise.

It was an animal hide of some kind, with wings, head, and claw-tipped paws attached to it, and underneath it was a long black gown of the style that Grahame himself wore. Grahame pushed the skin garment back from the man's shoulders, then, holding the head on his knee, he began to ease off the beast-mask. He was muttering all the time, broken, indistinguishable words, and as the mask came free Adam leaned eagerly forward to look at the face beneath it. Grahame's body blocked his view. He dropped to his knees beside the body, then drew back in astonishment and horror as Grahame exclaimed,

"He is alive! God be praised, he is still alive!"

Grahame's voice was a sob. His hands, gently stroking, caressed the Devil's face; then carefully, like a mother laying a child down, he lowered the Devil's head to the ground again. He looked up at Adam and Gilly. The blue light from the horse fell on his face, and on that of the motionless form beside him, and *they were the same face*—feature for feature, line for line the same!

Adam stared, feeling nightmare closing in on him, stifling his breath, contracting the world to a patch of ghastly blue light with two identical faces floating hazily in it. The Devil and Master Grahame—Master Grahame and the Devil. But which was which? Whom were they to trust now? Was this what Master Grahame had meant when he said the Devil and the Grand Master were one and the same person? But how could one man have two bodies, how could—

Adam's thoughts scattered in blind confusion. Gilly's hand fell on his shoulder. Gilly's voice moaned,

"He is a warlock—he must be a warlock! There is witchcraft of some kind here and we have been trapped by it."

Master Grahame made to rise, his mouth opening for speech; but Adam forestalled him, leaping in panic to his feet and yelling,

"Stand off, warlock, or I will scatter your brains with this other stone!"

"Have you never heard of identical twins before?"

Grahame's voice, sharp with scorn, arrested his hand swinging up with the other stone clenched in it. He gaped stupidly, and Grahame pressed on,

"I have not trapped you, and 'tis no witchcraft you see now. I am still Gideon Grahame, the alchemist, as I have always been, and this man here is my twin brother, Richard."

Adam let the hand with the stone in it drop slowly down. Wonderingly he looked again from the immobile face of Richard Grahame to the tormented copy that Gideon Grahame raised to him.

"Now you know what I was hiding from you," the alchemist told him bitterly. "Are you satisfied, Adam, or do you want to know what bred my secret?"

Adam shaped a soundless "Aye, sir," and Gideon Grahame looked down again at Richard Grahame. "We grew up together in Edinburgh," the bitter voice went on, "both with a passion for knowledge, our minds and feelings intertwined as only those of identical twins can be. But Richard's passion was different from mine. I wanted knowledge for its own sake, for the joy of discovery. Richard wanted knowledge for the power it could give him, and so while I pursued the path of true philosophy, he turned to the black arts. And he became an adept at them. He became famous!"

Master Grahame glanced up again, his lips twisting in self-mockery. "I correct myself—he became notorious; a man to be hated yet feared, a man who could claim some of the highest in the land as his clients and did not scruple to blackmail them for protection against the law. And I? I became a laughing-stock in Edinburgh, constantly mistaken in the streets for my notorious twin, always in danger of prison for my likeness to him, my scholarly credit destroyed, my name suspect, my friends abused for consorting with me. And so I went into exile, burying myself in Tranent village and pursuing my researches in loneliness and bitterness for thirty long years. But there is no time or distance that can break the bond between the minds of identical twins—as I have found to my great cost."

"How so, sir?" Adam found his voice at last, and Gilly, murmuring pitifully beside him, asked the same question.

"Richard needed me," Gideon Grahame said wearily. "He needed to boast of his foul exploits, and I was the only one to whom he could safely do so. He wrote to me of them from time to time, and so I knew he was masquerading as the Devil. The rest of my knowledge of witchcraft was remembered from early days with him and I added to this by studying the records of witch-trials, collecting case after case to compare with what I had already learned. I felt myself somehow driven to do so, for I was never free of my brother's presence—never!"

Grahame had begun to talk more to himself now than to Adam and Gilly. His gaze becoming unfocused, he went on,

"Thirty years I have lived in his shadow, knowing him still a part of me, feeling him here inside my breast like my own heart beating. He dogs my every step like another self, so that sometimes I wonder if he *is* myself; an embodiment of all the evil of which I am capable—a dark side of my soul, maybe, that dare not face God? And sometimes this clouds my mind so that I think I will go mad wondering if it is really so. I . . ."

His voice trailed into silence, then abruptly, he re-focused on Adam and Gilly and said quietly, "He is my enemy. He built his life at the expense of destroying mine. Yet still I love my brother, my enemy, for we are still two halves of the one whole, and nothing can alter that. You must accept this, even if you cannot understand it. And now, to work."

Bending to the figure on the ground he unloosed the pouch at its girdle and drew something from inside it—a six-inch-high wax model of a man, blood-stained, a strip of paper bound with black thread around its middle. The figure was well-made, every detail of it carefully shaped, from the face with its high forehead and pointed beard down to the wrinkles around the knees of the hose and the buckles on the shoes. For several shocked moments all three of them stared in silence at it, then Grahame threw it disgustedly down and ground it to fragments under his heel.

The figure on the ground stirred and moaned, and without waiting for instruction, Adam darted away to fetch the rope. The prisoner's eyes were open when he returned with it, but he was still dazed and only came fully to his senses as Master Grahame commanded,

"Tie him firmly, Adam."

"Brother Gideon! What on earth—Was it *you* who attacked me?" Richard Grahame struggled to rise with the words, but as he achieved a sitting position, Adam dropped a noose of the rope neatly over his shoulders and pulled it tight around his upper arms. Another half dozen swift turns of the rope had his arms pinned firmly to his sides, and with the rest of it brought down to tie around his ankles Adam had him secure. Rolling the prisoner aside then, he retrieved the animal disguise and handed it to Master Grahame.

Richard Grahame stopped his protesting and swearing at this point and stared at his brother. He was breathing hard, and the veins of his face were swollen with rage, but he spoke evenly.

"Well, brother Gideon, will you tell me now the meaning of all this?"

"'Tis very simple, Richard." Gideon Grahame also kept his voice even. "I learned of the plot that you and Bothwell had made against the King, and determined to stop it. This I have done by destroying the wax image I took from your pouch. And so that you will not be able to encourage the witch-covens to attempt the King's life again, I propose now to destroy your authority over them."

"Gideon, you are a fool; you always were a fool!" Richard Grahame chuckled grimly. "How do you suppose you can destroy the authority of the Devil over the witches!"

Gideon Grahame held up the animal disguise. "Easily," he answered. "Tonight I shall preside over the Sabbat in your place, wearing your disguise; and I shall ruin your credit with the witches there by confessing to them that the plot has failed *because the Devil's power is not strong enough to make it succeed!* Your reign is already at an end, Richard."

"They will see through the imposture!" Richard Grahame exclaimed.

"Why should they? They never saw through your imposture."

"There is one who knows the truth of it. He will unmask you, and then throw you to the witches to tear to pieces."

"Dr. Fian, your Registrar?" Gideon Grahame smiled. "But how would he know the difference between us, Richard, even if he did unmask me? And how could he guess that Gideon Grahame is your twin when you have driven me into exile so close that he has never even seen my face before?"

"How do you know Fian is my Registrar? Who told you?" Richard Grahame turned his head swiftly to peer at Adam and Gilly. "These two? But the boy is not one of ours, and the girl—yes, the girl is! I know her. I have known that big-eyed

brat since she was eleven years old. But she will suffer for this!
Do you hear that, girl?"

He glared at Gilly, face contorted into a snarling threat.
"You will die for this, Gilly Duncan, and so will this interfer-
ing brother of mine."

"No." Gideon Grahame moved to lay his arm protectively
across Gilly's shoulders. "I have promised to save this child
from your vengeance, Richard, and I shall. Nor do I intend
to fall victim to it, and so I have engaged passages for Gilly and
myself on a ship that sails from these shores by to-morrow
afternoon's tide. Our fate will not be yours to settle, brother,
but our own."

"And what of mine?" Richard Grahame enquired satiri-
cally. "I suppose you have plans for me too, brother! What is
it to be, eh? The King's justice? The torture chamber and
then a fiery death?"

A spasm of pain crossed Gideon Grahame's face. "You will
burn in the end without any help from me," he answered, and
then turned to Adam, drawing a kerchief from the pocket of
his gown.

"Gag him with this," he said quietly, "then drag him into
the wood. He will be found there when daylight comes and
that is ample time for our purpose. Give me at least ten
minutes start after that so that I can arrive at the Sabbat well
ahead of you. Then if by any chance Fian does discover my
imposture, you will be warned by the uproar that is bound
to follow."

Reluctantly, thinking of Richard Grahame's threat that the
witches would tear his brother in pieces, Adam took the
kerchief, and Master Grahame told Gilly,

"Remember, child, the tide will not wait. You must be at
Prestonpans harbour by noon to-morrow, or I will have to leave
without you."

"You are dangering your life enough for me, sir," she
answered gravely. "I will not expect more of you."

Master Grahame prepared to fit the animal mask over his
head, then hesitated, glancing down to his double lying bound
in the roadway. Quietly, with deep sadness in his voice, he said,

"Good-bye—brother."

He waited a moment but no answer came, and suddenly

appearing to gather resolution, he completed the gesture of assuming the Devil's guise. Gilly put the reins of the fiery horse into the claws that covered his hands, and swinging into the saddle he urged the beast off at a gallop into the darkness.

Chapter 8

SABBAT

The church and hospice of Saint Andrew, patron saint of sailors, had been appropriately built on the rocky off-shore islet of Longbelland, whence the little town of North Berwick sent out its ferry-boats to the opposite shore of the Firth of Forth. There was a bridge connecting the island to the spur of rock which formed the tip of the mainland, but North Berwick itself lay at the inland end of this spur and the church was further isolated by the high wooden stockade surrounding the town.

The witches, in fact, as Master Grahame had pointed out to Adam, had been most cunning in their choice of a site for the Hallowe'en Sabbat, for this one would not only provide them with a Christian church to desecrate. Out there on the island they would be completely hidden from the townsfolk, and on Hallowe'en especially, any noise of revelry from such a lonely place would only serve to terrorise those unlucky enough to hear it.

Cautiously riding Master Grahame's horse along the narrow lane outside the town's eastern boundary, Adam remembered these comments and wondered if indeed there was anyone awake and listening behind the palisade sliding by on his left. But Gilly was forging ahead on the mount they had previously shared, and he could not afford to dawdle over such speculations. Hurrying, he caught up with her as she turned the north-eastern corner of the stockade. The islet of Longbelland loomed up before them, black against the grey waters of the Firth of Forth, with the tower of the sailors' church pointing a finger of deeper black into the night sky.

Gilly set her mount to a path the kelp-carriers had beaten out in harvesting the seaweed from the jumble of rocks on the foreshore, and in single file they rode along it. A hum of noise from the Sabbat reached them as they began crossing the bridge between the mainland and the island. They made for the travellers' hospice standing directly behind the tower of the church, hearing single voices, yells, bursts of laughter, breaking through the general pattern of the noise. Adam tethered the horses in the lee of the hospice wall, and stood nervously adjusting his face-mask. Gilly touched his arm.

"Good fortune, Adam," she whispered, then walked boldly out from the shadows to the entrance gate in the churchyard wall.

It was only sensible, of course, that they should seem to arrive thus separately at the Sabbat; and apart from this, Adam realised, Gilly would certainly be quicker to note anything amiss in the gathering than he would be. Yet still it went against the grain to let her go first into danger, and the thirty seconds start they had agreed on seemed suddenly too long to him.

He counted them off, heart thudding at a rate that almost deafened him to the noise from the far side of the churchyard wall. At the count of thirty he straightened from his crouched position and forced himself to walk boldly forward as Gilly had done. With only a moment's hesitation at the entrance to the churchyard, he pushed the gate open and stepped forward. The full impact of the Sabbat burst on him, and he stopped short in his tracks, gaping at the scene.

The churchyard seethed with movement, like a giant cauldron bubbling—people dancing, people milling back and forth in small groups or large ones. Horses wandered among the tombstones, placidly cropping, and on the grass between the stones, also, bands of witches feasted like vultures among the dead. Single figures reeled from one picnicking group to another, yelling greetings, joining hoarsely in snatches of song, and on the fresh wind from the sea Adam smelled the heavy scent of malt liquor.

A man staggered past him breathing fumes of the liquor, and close behind the man came two masked women, protesting angrily.

"It is the rule at the Sabbat," the first of them screamed.

"Only false names can be used for fear of spies. And well you know that!"

The second woman caught viciously at the man's arm, shouting, "And your bye-name is Rob the Rowar, though you are too drunk to remember it!"

"And I must be called Cane," the first woman insisted, catching hold of the man's other arm.

"And my bye-name is Naip," the second woman added, shaking the man. "Remember that, you fool!"

The man dragged his arm free, staggering against Adam. "'Twas only a slip of the tongue, Mistress McCalzean," he defended himself, and the first woman screamed,

"There you go again, you great gomeril!"

Both women closed on him, striking out with their nails at his face, and like a hare bolting from its form, Adam fled the melée. His flight took him blundering into the antic dancing of another witch-group, and they struck out at him, yelling a mixture of threats and jeers at his clumsiness. He gasped, then staggered at the impact of an arm thrust across his chest.

In panic, he turned to run again, and was seized around the waist from behind. A hot breath fanned liquor-fumes into his nostrils. A voice yelled in his ear,

"Form the ring, damn you! Form the ring!"

From all sides followed a shout of "The ring! The ring!" A masked figure loomed up in front of Adam, the spare neat figure of a small man carrying himself straight as a ruler.

"The ring!" Dr. Fian's voice said crisply, and with the meaning of the words penetrating at last, Adam reached for the waist of the person nearest him. The woman, Cane, tagged on behind Dr. Fian. Figures rushed to add to the chain. A note of music vibrated from somewhere and a chorus of voices swelled up as Dr. Fian stepped off into the dance.

Commer goe ye before . . . Dr. Fian's neat figure was dancing towards the scattered tombstones. *Commer goe ye* . . .

To his horror, Adam realised that the cavorting figure he was clasping by the waist was that of Rob the Rowar, and gripped desperately at the cloth of the doublet under his hands. It was the direst bad luck to break the chain, Gilly had warned, and the witches would exact their own penalty from him if he let this wildly-leaping figure from under his hands.

Gif ye will not goe before, commer let me ...

Dr. Fian was leading the long chain of dancers round and round, in and out, weaving a complicated pattern through the tombstones, centring his pattern on a girl perched on one great crumbled stone. The girl's hands were held to her mouth. The vibrating notes of music that accompanied the song came from her, twanged out on a jews' harp. It was Gilly playing for the witches' song, and Adam recognised her with relief at her continued safety mixing with revulsion at her role in the dance.

Dr. Fian was headed for the porch at the west end of the church, now, and his arrival there gave the signal for the dance to end. The witches crowded forward to him as he mounted the steps of the porch. He paused at the top of the steps, and from some niche there produced the great black book of his office. The babble of the witches hushed as he stood holding it aloft.

"Servants of Satan," Dr. Fian cried, "you are about to meet your master. See that you keep his law!"

He turned towards the door of the church. It was made to open inwards from its centre, and with a single gesture he pushed the two halves of it wide apart. Adam was carried forward with the surge of witches following Dr. Fian into the darkness beyond the door, and felt his stomach heave in protest at the foul stench that reached him from a row of sulphur candles burning blue on the south side of the church.

The candles were ranged along the front edge of the pulpit standing tall and square between two pillars of the southern aisle, and in the uncertain light they cast he peered frantically around for Gilly. She was nowhere to be seen and the press of the crowd was sweeping him across the nave to the church's north aisle. His hand encountered a pillar and he clung to it, determined to be in a position to protect his back if he had to stand and defend himself.

A dull thud announced the shutting of the church doors, and at the sound, all conversation among the witches ceased abruptly. The blue candle-flames edging the pulpit fluttered wildly, dipped low, then sprang up again; and as the flames flared tall, the Devil appeared suddenly behind them. With one accord the witches sank to their knees, heads dipping to the presence in the pulpit like a field of barley bending low in the wind; and with one accord they moaned,

Master, master, master ...

On his knees on the cold stone of the church floor, Adam tried to still his galloping heart by reminding himself that this thing with the beast-face towering above him was only Master Grahame in disguise, and that Master Grahame had as much cause to fear these debased, moaning wretches as Gilly and himself. He rose with the others as the Devil took the black book of office Fian handed up to him and laid it open on the reading ledge of the pulpit.

"Hoodikin!" the Devil called, and a woman's voice answered, "Here, master."

"Reiver!"

"Here, master," a second voice answered.

"Thief of hell ... Greymeill ... Lightfoot ... Cane ... Prickeare ... Littleman ... Barrebon ... Naip..." The roll-call of nicknames continued, with each witch answering in turn, "Here, master."

"Elva!"

Adam looked around again for Gilly, noting that an old man in front of him had answered to the name, Greymeill, and that Cane and Naip were a few yards away to his left with the tall, masked woman who had answered to "Elva" standing between them. Someone behind him tugged the back of his shirt with a gentle but deliberate action. He froze, willing himself not to turn his head, and after a moment a girl edged slowly forward to stand beside him.

"Janicot!"

"Here, master," the girl beside Adam answered in Gilly Duncan's light, clear voice, and his tenseness relaxed.

"Stay close now," he whispered, snatching a sideways look at her, and Gilly nodded in reply.

"Mutchkin ... Red-habit ... Aspic ... Mamillion ... Meal-poke..." The Devil came to the end of the long, fantastic roll-call. He closed the book and handed it down to Dr. Fian.

"Confess to me now, my servants," his voice boomed through the church. "What evil have you done?"

A clamour of voices broke out and was stilled again by his uplifted arms. In a mocking parody of a priestly voice he intoned,

"I confess..."

I confess... the witches responded in unison, and continued immediately with their separate confessions of evil. Voice strove against voice to be heard above the general din. Shriek competed against shriek, shout against shout, and through the rising roar of sound Adam heard snatches of the individual confessions.

...and blasted his crops ... a powerful spell to make her child sicken ... caused the cow to run dry ... poisoned ... tongue of an unchristened child ... laid a madness on him ... bewitched ...

The catalogue of deeds went on and on, with the witches seeming to take a dreadful joy in shouting their confessions aloud. The very thought of it all sickened Adam. He leaned against his pillar, trying to close his ears to the insistent confessions, but was jerked to attention again by a woman's scream rising suddenly higher than the rest of the voices.

"Where is the image that he promised us?"

A concerted shout came from the people nearest the woman who had screamed. "Aye, give us the image, master!"

Gilly tugged agitatedly at Adam's sleeve and indicated the tall woman call Elva. Reaching up to put her lips to Adam's ear, she hissed,

"That big woman is Agnes Sampson. 'Twas she who cried out about the image."

The unison shout from those around Agnes Sampson had beaten down some of the babble from the rest of the witches, and their voices faltered still further when she led her group in a repetition of the yell,

"Where is the image, master?"

The woman, Cane, screamed, "And when is the King to die?"

Greymeill, the old man standing in front of Adam, turned a puzzled look on Cane and called out, "What d'ye mean, woman? The King is well and hearty, thank God!"

Adam craned eagerly to hear what Cane's answer might be, then jerked back again as another man—drunken Rob the

Rowar—swung round to give Greymeill a great buffet on the face and yell,

"The King is an enemy to witches, you old fool!"

Greymeill cowered, but other voices took up his cry. Other witches crowded forward to the group around Agnes Sampson. This, Adam guessed, must be made up only of the covens who had held the Esbat at Aitchison's Haven, for the rest of the witches seemed as ignorant of the wax image plot as old Greymeill and there was a growing menace in the din of questions they were directing at Agnes Sampson.

"Ask him up there!" Her powerful voice rose, screaming, above the noise. "Ask the Master what image this is and what it has to do with the King!"

The mob swayed, all heads turning to look up at the pulpit, all sound dying to a quarrelsome mutter. The beast-headed creature in the pulpit stared impassively down on the mass of upturned faces. Agnes Sampson's arm shot up from among them, her finger pointed in challenge at the Devil.

"Let him speak!" she screamed. "He promised us a wax image of the King to roast in the fire, and so enchant the King to his death. He promised he would help us kill the King!"

In the deathly hush that followed her words Adam's gaze glided from face to face among the witches, and his heightened senses told him the thoughts behind their startled expressions.

To lay a spell that would destroy a neighbour's crops, to make his cow run dry, or his children sicken—that was the common run of witchcraft and they would perform it without a qualm, with malicious pleasure, in fact. But to kill the King —that was almost like trying to kill God! The King, after all, was divinely appointed to rule the land. He was God's vice-regent on earth! They stared, dumbly trying to grasp the thought of an evil so daring, and the Devil's voice boomed out over their frightened staring.

"Then I promised what I had no power to perform, woman, for the King is a man of God."

"But you are God's adversary," Agnes Sampson shouted, and contemptuously the Devil answered her protest,

"Do you not know your Bible, woman? Is it not written there that God will protect His own from His adversary? A fine witch you are if you have not yet learned that the Devil can harm only those who have already wandered from God's side!"

"So you have lied to us!" Agnes Sampson shrieked with rage and shook both her fists at him. "You lied!"

"I lied, I lied!" the Devil mimicked her shriek. "Of course I lied, woman. *The Devil is the father of lies!*"

The beast-head went back, yelling with laughter at its own black humour, and the awed silence of the witches broke into laughter also. They tittered at first, hands cupped over mouths, then, encouraged by the beast's ferocious mirth, they too yelled, and scornfully pointed at the furious gestures of Agnes Sampson and her group. Adam stood breathless at the sheer effrontery of the tactics Master Grahame had used, and looked down at Gilly's excited tug on his sleeve.

"The others hate Sampson, but they are afraid of her too," she told him rapidly. "That is why they are so glad to see the Devil make a jest of her."

But no-one there would ever trust the Devil's word again, Adam thought grimly. And never again would they believe he could help them bewitch the King or any other godly man to his death. The second stage of Master Grahame's plan had been successful. He had broken his brother's hold over the witches. But there was still the third stage: Gilly's escape from their vengeance; and the first step in that was up to him. He looked around, calculating his moves.

The witches were still riding high on the crest of their satisfied spite at Agnes Sampson, and the Devil had yet more diversion in store for them. Leaning over the pulpit, he shouted,

"Hear me now, hear the word of the foul fiend himself, for there is more yet to be done on this Sabbat! You need the bones of dead men to grind into powder for your spells, their fat to make ointments, their shrouds for talismans. And so, out, I say! Out into the churchyard with me to break open graves and make the dead work for Satan and his servants!"

"Out! Out and make the dead work!" the witches yelled in response. Dr. Fian moved to open the doors of the church again, and Adam made up his mind. The roll-call, after all, had proved Gilly's attendance at the Sabbat, and she was not likely to be missed in the drunken festivities that would follow the opening of the graves. Gripping her arm he whispered,

"Edge back behind the pillar, Gilly. 'Tis time for us to go."

He suited the action to the word, drawing Gilly with him. The rest of those in the church were in motion also, surging towards the door in a struggling mass. Adam's steady pressure freed himself and Gilly of the immediate press around them. They slid behind the shelter of the pillar and stood pressed against it, listening to the voices in the church rise to a crescendo of excitement and then begin to fade again as the witches poured out into the churchyard. Adam waited until he judged they would all be hard at work breaking open the graves; then peering out from behind the pillar, he surveyed the church. It lay quiet and apparently empty in the guttering light of the pulpit candles, but there could be watchers in the shadows and there was no point in Gilly as well as himself being caught.

"Wait here," he told her, and made a quick, silent-footed sortie across the nave to the west door. From the shadow of the porch there, he stared out into the churchyard.

The witches already had one grave opened, and they were dragging a body from it. The Devil was perched aloft on the tombstone at the head of the grave, black wings spread, body crouched like that of some huge bird of prey stooping for the kill, and with horror, Adam heard his yells of encouragement to the witches. Master Grahame, he thought, was playing his part well—too well! Then remembering that the lives of all three of them hung on the success of the impersonation, was ashamed of his own squeamishness.

A glance to his right showed him a group of witches capering around another open grave near the gate in the churchyard wall. There could be no escape by that route, he realised, and returned silently to where he had left Gilly hiding behind the pillar.

"There is no escape by way of the west door," he told her. "Is there any other way out of the church?"

"In the tower," she whispered. "A small door that opens towards the hospice."

She led the way, guiding him with a handhold along the darkness of the aisle behind the row of pillars and through an archway into the tower. On the far side of the tower she fumbled with the latch of a small door. It creaked open under her hand at last, to show the wall of a building a few feet beyond it. Adam followed her through the doorway, recognising the building as the hospice behind the church, and saw the horses grazing peacefully where he had left them in the lee of the hospice wall.

"Walk them across the bridge—slowly," he whispered to Gilly, "then mount, and ride like the wind."

It was the last word that either of them spoke before they reached Master Grahame's house again that night, but after the first mile, when they had ceased to look behind them, their silence was a companionable one. Adam glanced occasionally at Gilly, wondering if she found it as hard to believe as he did that it was all over, and that to-morrow would see the beginning of a new life for her. He would miss her, he realised, and would have told her so if he could have found the words to frame the thought.

At the stable behind Master Grahame's house she slid wearily down from the saddle and asked, "Shall I help you with the horses, Adam?"

"No need." He looked at the tired droop of her shoulders and added, "Get to bed. To-morrow is also a day."

She gave a little laugh, the first real laugh he had ever heard from her. "I shall miss you, Adam," she told him, and turned to trudge homewards.

Unharnessing the horses, rubbing them down, Adam thought how pleasant the words had sounded, and how simple, after all, to say: *I shall miss you.* He whistled softly, enjoying the feeling of work well done, and wondered where Master Grahame had left the fiery horse tethered during the Sabbat. In some stable provided by Dr. Fian, very likely, he decided; otherwise, they would have seen its light. And after the Sabbat, it would be easy for Master Grahame to discard both his disguise and the phosphorescent covering on the horse so that he could ride home undetected. There was nothing further to worry about—not a single thing. Every part of the scheme was complete now, exactly as they had planned it in all those long conversations in Master Seton's dove-cote.

The long night began to have its effects, and he was sleepy

when he left the stable at last. Head down, eyes threatening to close at every step he took, he plodded homewards and turned wearily into the archway leading to the stable-yard.

They were on him before he had taken two steps along the passage under the arch—two men bearing him down with their weight, so that his head cracked against the cobbles. Hands pinioned his arms. A knee thudded down on his chest. There was a man's weight behind the knee pressing into him, and a voice exclaiming,

"Got you! Got you at last, Adam Lawrie!"

It was Jardine's voice, Jardine snarling triumphantly, and it was answered by another, the fawning voice of Dod Carnegie.

"Aye, you've waited a long time for this moment!"

Jardine chuckled, and unbelievingly through his daze Adam heard him answer, "But it was worth it, to catch him *and* the girl in the end!"

Chapter 9

TORTURE

There was a sound of screaming from the great hall of Master Seton's house. Adam heard it as Jardine and Carnegie tossed him down on the kitchen floor, and he struggled up again, tugging at the rope they had used to tie his hands behind his back. Breathlessly he demanded of Jardine,

"What goes on in there?"

Dod Carnegie grinned foolishly. Jardine's eyes slid gloatingly to the wall between the kitchen and the great hall.

"What goes on?" he repeated. "Why, a meeting of the Town Council to examine the witch, Gilly Duncan, of course."

Another outburst of screaming filtered through the dividing wall, and in a frenzy of tugging at his bonds Adam shouted,

"They are torturing her! Oh, my God, stop—tell them to stop it!"

"Stop?" Jardine mocked. "They are only at the beginning of it. That will be the pilliwinks they are trying, and once they have screwed these tight enough to break her thumbs they will likely go on to the rope."

"The rope?" Adam stopped struggling to stare at him.

Grinning, Jardine assured him, "'Tis a good device! They take a piece of fine, strong cord, you see, and tie knots in every inch or so of its length. Then they will cut off her hair and draw the knotted rope tight round her head till the pain of it makes her answer everything she is asked."

Adam blundered his way to a bench and let himself slump on to it. His legs still trembled. He looked down at them dully as he decided he would kill Jardine. But there were more questions yet to be answered. He looked up again.

"How long?" he asked quietly. "How long have you been spying on us, Jardine?"

"Since the night she doctored your back for you," Jardine boasted. "You never suspected that, did you, gallows-brat? But I saw her slipping across the yard that night. I heard what she told you then, and so I waited and I watched till I saw her going out at night again alone—three times I saw her. Then she went out on the night of the great storm, and you followed her, and again I waited and I watched till I saw the two of you go out together at night."

He paused to give Adam a chance to speak, but the denial he was plainly hoping for did not come, and after a moment he continued,

"You were very thick with one another after that—always down at the dove-cote together, always little looks and signs passing between you. But it was when you went out together again—tonight of all nights—that I knew I had you for my own! I woke Master Seton with the news that I had discovered two witches in his household, and he is not the man to stomach that. By the time Gilly arrived back here tonight, he had the Town Council summoned all ready to examine her, *and you are next on the list!*"

"I am no witch," Adam told him, "and there is nothing but your word to say that Gilly is one."

"So you think!" Jardine mocked. "But you are wrong, for she carries a witch-mark on her shoulder, and that is proof positive she is signed to the Devil."

A memory of Gilly's voice echoed in Adam's mind. *Then the Devil pricked my shoulder with something sharp like a bod-kin that left a blue mark on the skin....* He looked up, his eyes narrowing.

"How do you know she carries a witch-mark?"

"Because I have seen it!" Jardine flung at him. "She would not let Mistress Tait search her for the Devil's sign, and so I held her while Master Seton ripped the gown off her back. And I saw it then, on her shoulder."

Dod Carnegie laughed, a sly, sniggering laugh. The screams from the other side of the wall rose in pitch and volume. In a burst of despairing fury Adam heaved himself to his feet and rushed at his jailers, kicking, butting, thrusting out with his shoulders in a wild attempt to inflict some sort of injury on them. They leaped out of his way and circled him tauntingly, jeering, hooting with laughter, till Jardine brought the baiting to an end with a blow from Mistress Tait's bittling-stick.

The heavy wooden stave cracked against Adam's skull, and sent him reeling across the kitchen to crash down on his back. The rafters of the ceiling spun like dark wheel-spokes above him, spun with a high, screaming noise. The scream faded to a gnat's whine; died. The wheel diminished to a spinning black dot; vanished...

Adam came very slowly back to his senses. The kitchen was quiet. He struggled up to lean on one elbow, trying to place the sound that was missing, and remembered the screaming. It had stopped now. Dod Carnegie was looking down at him, a faint curiosity replacing his usual expression of stupid slyness.

"Gilly...?" Adam managed thickly.

"She has confessed," Dod said.

His voice, the grin he gave, were nervous. He nodded, his sly face growing solemn as he added for emphasis,

"The witch has confessed."

The news penetrated slowly to Adam's dazed mind. "Help me up," he muttered.

Dod surveyed him, saw there was no fight left in him, and helped him up to sit on the bench again.

"You took a sore dunt on your head there," he remarked.

"Aye," Adam muttered. "Aye." He waited for his spinning head to clear, gathering his thoughts painfully from all their scattered corners and finding no comfort in them.

If Gilly had confessed to witchcraft against the King, she was doomed. But what about himself? He would be equally doomed by his attendance at the Sabbat. And Master Grahame, too! He would be arrested in the general witch-hunt that would follow Gilly's confession; and how could either of them hope to prove their innocence in such a panic atmosphere?

Adam looked slowly up at the vacant eyes watching him and wondered how much Dod Carnegie knew about Gilly's confession. It would be worth trying to find out, he decided, and cautiously advanced his opening remark.

"Gilly never did harm to anyone that I know of."

He glanced up at Dod again. "She never harmed you, did she, Dod?"

"No." Dod agreed. He pondered the thought, and argued with himself, "Right enough, she never did. There was no malice at all in her."

Adam opened his eyes wide in exaggerated surprise. "Then what could such a harmless wee lass have to confess?"

Dod snorted. "You may ask! Jardine heard her telling it all, and he says—" He leaned closer to Adam, licking his lips in anticipation of his own words, then suddenly drew back again and blurted, "But I was not to tell you."

"Please yourself, Dod." Adam shrugged, pretending indifference. "But you will not convince me that a quiet soul like Gilly has anything worth confessing. You are just inventing it all, to blow up your own importance."

"I am not," Dod protested. "Why do you think there has been all this fuss—the Town Council turned out of their beds and all—if there was nothing to be discovered in the long run?"

Adam laughed. "A few silly old women dancing widdershins round a bonfire, maybe," he said scornfully, "and Gilly there to fetch and carry for their feasting. That is all they would find! You are a fool to believe anything else."

"'Tis you who are the fool," Dod retorted. "Jardine told me—"

He caught himself up abruptly again, and Adam plunged in, "Stuff! Jardine treads on you like he treads on dirt. He would not tell you anything."

"He did too," Dod flared out at him. "He told me that she has named every one of the witches who were out this Hallowe'en—above seven-score of them, he said. And they were no harmless carlins, these ones, for they had a plot to kill the King!"

"Gilly said that!" Adam tried to make his tone incredulous. "But Dod, if she has named all these witches, then she has cleared me, for *I* am no witch and *I* never plotted to kill the King. Did she not say so?"

"Aye, she did," Dod said in a puzzled voice. "That is the queer thing about it all. You were with her at this witches' gathering, and yet she says—" He paused to eye Adam curiously, and then finished, "She says it was because you were trying to put a stop to all this plotting."

"Single-handed?" Adam probed.

"Aye, that is what she says, but Jardine told me that Master Seton means to question you separately, and then—"

The intent expression on Adam's face suddenly penetrated Dod's dim mind. He gulped, realising at last the extent of his indiscretion, and backed a step.

"I—oh, my God," he muttered, then burst out with almost comic woe, "Jardine will kill me for this!"

"Ach, away!" Adam dismissed his alarm. "I will not say a word about it to him or to anyone else, Dod. And you can rest easy in your own mind, for I swear to you it is the truth I am no witch."

Dod mumbled some confused reply. He sidled to the door, from whence he continued to cast uneasy looks in Adam's direction, but Adam was too lost in thought now to notice him. Frowning, staring into space, he considered the information he had gathered.

If Dod had told him correctly, he decided, then Gilly had somehow managed to avoid any mention of Master Grahame in her confession. And that meant he would get clean away as they had planned! Also, it seemed she had done her utmost to save himself from the fate that she was bound to suffer. But how much of torture had she been forced to endure in order to protect them so?

Adam bowed his head, stifling a groan at the recollection of the terrible screaming he had heard. And yet still, after all that, she must burn! There was no hope of saving a confessed witch from the law—more especially a witch who had been concerned in the attempted murder of the King! Unless— Adam's mind began to race with an idea.

Gilly had provided the chance to prove his own innocence. Could he not build on that? Supposing the chance succeeded —could he not pretend he had acted out of loyalty to the King as well as in order to help her? That would gain him credit on all sides, and he could surely use that credit on her behalf? Supposing he—

"Hey, Adam!" Dod Carnegie's voice broke into his train of thought. He looked up to see the kitchen door ajar, with

Dod standing by it in a listening attitude. "I can hear someone coming to the door of the hall," Dod hissed.

Adam rose to his feet. Dod came a step or two towards
him and said hurriedly,

"'Tis Jardine. I know his tread. But mind you, now! Not
a word about my tongue running away with my wits."

"Trust me," Adam assured him, and wondered at the
stupidity of the man. It would be so simple for him, after all,
to claim that his tattle had only been a crafty device to draw
the prisoner out; and to lie about the answers he had received
to it. It would be one word against another then, and neither
Jardine nor the Town Council would incline to take that of
a suspected witch! Adam gave silent thanks for Dod's fear of
Jardine. He braced himself to the sight of the kitchen door
swinging wide and the ferret-face of his enemy appearing in
the opening.

"You are for it now, gallows-brat!"

Jardine was there, grinning triumph at him. Jardine was
advancing, and ordering as he came, "Take his other arm,
Dod."

Their hands fastened on Adam's arms, and pushing him
before them they marched the few steps into the hall next
door. "The man-witch, sirs!" Jardine announced, and shoved
him forward in a stumbling rush that took him almost to the
dining-board at the other end of the room.

Adam had a fleeting impression of the Town Councillors
staring at him across the breadth of the board, their faces
drawn with lack of sleep, their robes shrugged on any which
way over doublets only half-laced. He righted his balance and
realised the presence of the Reverend Mr. Forrester in the
row of Councillors. An ashy-faced Mistress Tait sat bolt upright on a wooden settle at one end of the table. Master Seton
stood beside her, his bulky form almost obscuring that of
Gilly on the other half of the settle. No-one spoke, and almost
angrily Adam challenged the disapproval in the minister's
elderly face.

"I am no man-witch, but a baptised Christian, as you well
know."

"You are here to be examined on that very point," Seton
answered his challenge, and moved to resume his place among

the other Councillors. Deliberately then, Adam turned to look at Gilly.

She lay slumped against the arm of the settle, her eyes closed and her eyelids showing like great, plum-coloured bruises in the deathly paleness of her face. Her arms hung loosely in front of her, with the thumb of each hand splayed at a peculiar angle to the fingers. The thumbs were livid with bruising also, and so grotesquely swollen that they were more like monstrous growths than natural members; but it was her head, and not her mangled hands that held Adam's horrified attention.

The thick, fair hair, he saw, had been roughly cropped from it, and the tender skin of the scalp showed the mark of the rope-torture in a wide, encircling band of blood, from which little blood-encrusted spikes of hair stuck out like thorns. Speechless, his stomach heaving with revulsion for this thing that had been done to her, he stared at the slight form on the settle. Gilly lay so still that he could detect no sign of breathing from her, and his voice came out at last in a whisper of apprehension.

"Is she—dead?"

"Indeed, she is not," Master Seton answered impatiently. "We have but made her ripe for the burning; as you will also be if you do not answer this question truthfully. Have you forsworn your Christian baptism to the Devil?"

Adam jerked around to face him. "I have told you already! I am no witch. And I *hate* the Devil!"

"We will see." Master Seton looked along the row of Councillors. "I hope I know my duty, sirs, which is to say that I will not harbour witches in my house. You may search this servant of mine for witch-marks."

With a low mutter of comment passing among them, the Councillors shuffled to their feet and came to crowd around Adam. Hands fumbled the rope away from his wrists. Hands plucked at his shirt, his breeches, stripping them roughly away. Fingers poked and prodded at him, rasped over his skin, even searched the scalp under his thick hair.

"Nothing ... He is clear, Baillie ... not a blemish ..."

They left him to shrug into his clothes again, making their several reports as they returned to their places. With an effort,

Adam bit down his anger at the way he had been handled and waited for the next question.

"Come here, Adam." Seton beckoned him with a jewelled hand, and he stepped forward to the dining-board. "Now look at these." The jewels twinkled as Seton swept his hand along the board, indicating the items that lay on it: a pair of thumb-screws, a length of knotted rope stained darkly with blood, writing materials, and some sheets of paper covered with scrawled writing. His gaze met Adam's and grimly he continued,

"The pilliwinks and the rope are for you if you will not answer to Jardine's accusation that you are a witch, he having seen you in the company of the witch, Gilly Duncan, on certain nights and especially on this night of Hallowe'en. But take care to answer truthfully, for these sheets are Gilly's own confession of witchcraft, taken down at her dictation by the Town Clerk; and if what you have to say does not tally with that confession, then I will know that one or other of you is lying. Perhaps even both of you, so that we will have to put her to the torture again as well as you. Now, answer me—"

"A moment, sir," Adam interrupted, and all along the table astonished eyebrows were raised, but the plan in Adam's mind had taken definite shape now and he continued determinedly, "There will be no need of further torture, for I admit here and now that I have been in Gilly's company tonight and on other nights. And there will be no need of questions either, if you will let me make a statement in answer to the charge of witchcraft against me."

Seton withdrew his gaze doubtfully. The Councillor on his left whispered something to him, and the whispered conference extended along the length of the table. Heads nodded in agreement, and Seton looked up to give the general verdict.

"Very well. The Council allows, if you are prepared to swear an oath of truth on the Bible."

Adam glanced towards the massive Bible in front of the place occupied by Mr. Forrester. He would speak the truth, he promised himself; or at least such parts of it as could safely be spoken. As for what he meant to say about his loyalty to the King, surely God would forgive him telling such a harmless little lie in order to save Gilly's life?

"I will swear such an oath," he answered Seton, and moving to lay his right hand on the Bible said rapidly, "I swear on God's holy Word to speak the truth to all here present."

Mr. Forrester stroked his white Geneva bands piously. "And if you lie," he rejoined, "may your soul burn in hell as your body will burn on earth."

A throaty growl of "Amen!" came from the Councillors, and for a second Adam was shaken in his purpose. But he had already made his private peace with God, he reminded himself, and began boldly,

"I saw the Devil for the first time on Lammas Eve, and he was like a beast riding on a fiery horse. It was the light of his horse that attracted me abroad that night. It was about two weeks later that I learned Gilly was a witch, but I promised not to speak of it to anyone because she told me she was a witch unwilling, her mother having made her one, and she hated the Devil. Also, because she had been kind to me, and I knew her to be of gentle, harmless nature. Instead, I tried hard to persuade her to break with the witches, but she knew they would kill her if she did that, and so she would not be persuaded."

"Baillie..." Mr. Forrester leaned forward to Seton, indicating he had a question to ask, then looked at Adam and said,

"It was a mistaken kindness to keep such a sinful secret, but still a kindness and therefore understandable. But why did you not come to Master Seton in the first place and tell him you had seen the Devil?"

"I did think of doing so, sir," Adam admitted, "but I was afraid to speak for I thought he would not believe such a thing could happen and would simply have me whipped for night-prowling."

"Well, Baillie?" The minister sat back with a self-righteous air. "That seems to be a reflection on you, if your servant thinks you do not believe the Devil shows himself to mortal man!"

"No more than on you, reverend sir." Quickly Adam interposed before Seton could speak the angry reply hovering on his lips. "I also thought of telling you, but decided not to, for the very same reason."

"And *that* is not surprising," Seton remarked angrily. "You have been very slack in your Communion services these many years past, minister!"

The Town Clerk, a dry little man with the darting eyes of an inquisitive bird, said unexpectedly, "Indeed, 'tis no wonder the Devil wanders this parish to our great undoing!"

There was a murmur of agreement along the table. The minister flushed slightly, and in the disapproving looks that were cast at him, Adam read the signs of a tide that might yet turn in his favour. The Councillors were looking for a scapegoat for the evil they had uncovered in their midst, he realised, and every person proved innocent would show that their village had not been entirely corrupted. And Master Seton would be only too relieved to have at least part of the slur on his household proved false! With cautiously rising spirits he continued,

"I was curious about Gilly after that, sirs, and so I followed her when she went out one night—the night of the great storm at the end of harvest-time this year. I saw the witches meet the Devil that night, and I learned of their plot to kill the King by means of roasting his image in wax. This filled me with horror and I challenged Gilly on it, but she was in a cleft stick in the matter for she knew the witches would kill her if she betrayed them. Yet death by the justice-fire faced her also if she should be taken in the witch-hunt that would surely follow the success of their plot. Therefore, she could do nothing, although she was sore distressed that the King should die."

They were all following him closely, Adam noted, and so far it was evident he had not stumbled into saying anything that contradicted Gilly's confession. But now came his first real difficulty; yet surely if Gilly had managed to confess without making any mention of Master Grahame, he could also avoid doing so in the next part of his statement? Carefully choosing his words, he continued,

"I could see no help for it, sirs, but that Gilly must die, for I could not permit that the King be killed by witches. Yet still I pitied her, and so I persuaded her to go abroad from the house with me one night so that we could discuss the matter. That was the first occasion when Jardine saw us go out together, which I freely admit now to my own danger. Yet at the time I considered this danger to be well worth while, since it was from our discussion that night that we contrived a plan which we thought might save both Gilly *and* the King. This was to make an opportunity of destroying the wax image, so that it could not be burned by the witches as they had agreed they should do at their Sabbat in the kirk of North Berwick."

There was an exchange of looks among the Councillors. The Town Clerk picked up Gilly's confession and pointed out something in it to the Councillor seated next to him. The papers passed from hand to hand along the table, each man reading at the same place then looking thoughtfully at Adam before he passed it to his neighbour. Master Seton spoke, looking up in his turn.

"And so you went to this Sabbat tonight, with Gilly?"

"Yes, sir," Adam admitted. "That was the second time Jardine saw us go out together—but again I say I courted that danger for a good cause."

The Town Clerk spoke up again, inquisitive eyes peering. "Were you not afraid to go among all these witches?"

"I was very afraid, sir," Adam told him, and thought with relief that surely this question indicated they were beginning to accept the fact of his innocence. Now to build on that acceptance! He turned from the Clerk to face the full Council, and said frankly,

"And I would not have been able to overcome my fear if I had not known my cause to be good. For who is there here so base that he would not risk death for the sake of saving the King's life?"

The lie was out; it had almost stuck in his throat, but it was out at last! And surely, Adam argued to himself, it was not such a great lie to pretend to frankness and to suggest loyalty? With relief he noted the approving murmurs that had followed his words, and continued,

"And I have discovered, sirs, that even the Devil admits God will protect His own. For when the witches at the Sabbat clamoured to have the image, saying to the Devil he had promised to give it to them to be burnt, the Devil told them it was not in his power to kill the King because the King was a man of God. Whereat they cried out that he had lied to them, and he mocked them, saying that he had indeed lied, for the Devil is the father of lies. Then, seeing I could do no further good in the matter and believing all harm to have been removed from the King, I stole secretly away from the Sabbat with Gilly, and came home. That is all my statement, sirs, and now I commend myself to your justice, and to the justice of the King whom I have served faithfully, if not well."

The Town Clerk rose and left his place to whisper in Seton's ear. The minister rose to join them, and once again the whispered colloquy spread the length of the table. Seton brought it to an end by standing up with Gilly's confession in his hand.

"Gentlemen!" He held up the confession. "The statement just made by Adam Lawrie agrees with the substance of this confession made by Gilly Duncan, and each of these two having been questioned separately, the one therefore shows the other to be true. Therefore also, the accusation of witchcraft brought by Jardine against Adam Lawrie falls to the ground, for it follows that we are not dealing with two witches, but with one witch and a witness to her crimes."

"A witness who may have acted out of foolish kindness in one respect," the Town Clerk put in, "but who has still shown himself a good Christian and a loyal subject of the King."

He nodded approvingly to Adam, then turned to the minister. "Which speaks to his credit, reverend sir, and therefore also to the credit of this house, whatever you may think of Master Seton's beliefs about the Devil."

"Let us hope then," the minister retorted, "that having one such servant in his house will help Master Seton to avoid the ill-fame of having sheltered another who is a self-confessed witch!"

"I know my duty, I tell you!" Seton protested angrily. "She will not stay another moment under my roof now that her true nature is discovered; and by this time to-morrow, I promise you, she shall be burned."

"You go too fast, Davie, old friend," the Town Clerk reproved. "'Tis treason to plot the King's death, and a Town Council cannot pass sentence on treason."

"Indeed not!" the minister chimed in. "This is an affair of State, Master Seton, and only the King can pronounce on it—more especially as the witch has named the Earl of Both-well, the King's own cousin, as one of the guilty ones."

The Town Clerk scanned quickly along the listening faces of the other Councillors. "Are we agreed, then, that the person of this witch be surrendered to the King's justice?"

"Agreed!" The council chorused approval, and folding the pages of Gilly's confession Seton declared,

"Then I shall take her to the King myself, for 'tis both my right and my duty to do so."

"Sir!" Jardine called out. Under cover of the general hub-bub of conversation that had broken out he came forward to speak protestingly to Seton, and was told in a fierce under-tone.

"I will have enough to do to repair the good name of my house without any further pandering to your spite, Jardine. The lad is not only innocent; he has come out of the affair with some credit, so get away with you now."

Jardine moved unwillingly away, glaring baffled hatred at Adam as he passed, and Seton called after him,

"Saddle up a horse for me and one for Adam also, and be quick about it. We will ride straight for Edinburgh with the witch."

The Town Councillors rose in another flurry of chatter. Seton moved to the settle and Mistress Tait prepared to help Gilly to her feet, but he gripped her by the waist and slung her in a crumpled heap over his shoulder.

"Come, Adam!" he called, and strode to the door of the hall with Gilly's shorn and bloody head lolling over his shoulder and bobbing grotesquely at every step.

She had suffered such incredible pain to protect him, Adam thought, and for all this first success it was still only a slender hope he had of saving her now. He followed behind Master Seton, hardly able to bear the sight of Gilly's lolling head, and hoping desperately she would survive the ordeal of the ten-mile ride to Edinburgh.

Chapter 10

KING'S BARGAIN

It was not possible to wake the King with such a story at that hour, the Captain of the Guard informed them suspiciously when they reached Holyrood Palace at last. But Witchcraft Against His Majesty was a serious charge, of course, and if Master Seton wished to lay it before Lord Chancellor Thirlestane—? Master Seton had snatched at the reluctant offer, and with Captain Lauder still standing alertly by, had rehearsed his story to the Lord Chancellor.

Now, with a face as white as the napkin the Chancellor had called for to conceal her wounded head, Gilly stood swaying before the King's chair in the audience chamber of the royal suite. Captain Lauder continued to keep his careful watch over the odd party he had allowed into the Palace, and with one hand under Gilly's elbow in case she should fall, but with his attention temporarily distracted from her, Adam stood gaping from the high, vaulted ceiling of the audience chamber to the tapestries richly lining its walls.

It was not so large a room as he had expected from his first glimpse of the great, turreted pile that was the Palace itself, but still magnificent enough in his estimation, and the bed he could glimpse in the room beyond was hung with curtains that positively dazzled with their splendour of gold embroidery. His glance came back to touch briefly on the heavy-jowled face of the Lord Chancellor looming on the right of the dais that held the King's chair, and rested finally on the King himself.

Jamie Sixth, he thought curiously was not at all his idea of what a King should be. For one thing, he was not even dressed like a King—indeed, the velvet cap on his red hair was downright shabby. There were food-stains dribbled on to the ruff below his little, pointed red beard; down the front of his doublet also, and the toes of his shoes were scuffed. Nor did he look like a King, for all his lofty brow and long nose. He was more like a scholar, in fact, with that pale face and flabby body, and his loosely-drooping lower lip was surely not that of a man born to command. And he was so young! Not more than six or seven years senior to himself, Adam calculated, and found it hard to believe that this was the man who held not only Gilly's life, but the lives of all Scotland in his hand.

King James interrupted Master Seton's speech suddenly, in a peevish voice that matched Adam's poor estimate of him.

"Master Seton, I pray you pause for a moment to consider this. Francis Stewart is not only Earl of Bothwell, he is also Lord Crichton and Hailes, Sheriff of Liddesdale, and Lord Admiral of Scotland. Moreover, he is my own blood-cousin. Yet now you accuse this high nobleman of consorting with poor, debased rogues and conspiring with them to kill me by witchcraft and seize my throne, and 'tis only a very little witch you have brought with you in evidence of so grave a charge. Have you been well guided, sirrah, in forcing this tale upon me at such an early hour of the day? Do you not know it is a common matter for country maids like this child here to fancy they can cast spells and such-like foolishness?"

Adam noted the shrewdness in the heavy-lidded brown eyes fixed on Master Seton, and realised suddenly that this pale, flabby-looking young King was anything but a fool. Master Seton, he noted also, had been taken aback by this caution. With some of his self-importance gone and his hand trembling slightly as he held out Gilly's confession, he answered,

"Sire, I beg of you to read the witch's confession, writ by the hand of the Town Clerk of Tranent, and witnessed by the whole of the Town Council, as well as by the Reverend Alexander Forrester whose appointment to Tranent Parish Church was made at your own command. 'Tis the sworn word of all these honest men I bring with me in evidence, as well as the witch herself and this other servant of mine who witnessed her crimes."

The King's shrewd gaze rested briefly on Adam, then he took the confession that Seton held out and looked up at the tall, bearded figure of Lord Chancellor Thirlestane.

"Let Lord Bothwell be fetched from his lodgings in the Canongate," he ordered. "And at once, my Lord Chancellor."

"Sire!" Chancellor Thirlestane bowed before he stepped forward to scan the little knot of servants whispering together at the entrance to the audience chamber. His sharp little eyes singled out a young man with a smooth olive-skinned face and ringletted hair.

"French Paris!" he called, and beckoned.

The young man sauntered forward, insolence in every line of his foppishly-dressed figure and in the glance of his dark eyes.

"Your master is commanded by the King to present himself instantly," the Chancellor told him. "See to it, fellow."

"And Paris—" Without looking up from the confession held open in front of him, the King added to the order, "—bear in mind I have considered you ripe for a hanging for long enough now, and will indeed give the hangman his due if my Lord Bothwell does not obey me with speed."

"But Sire—" pettishly French Paris shook his ringlets as he began his protest.

King James looked up with a glance so brief that he could scarcely be said to have interrupted his reading, but there was that in his face which made French Paris gulp down the rest of his words and turn instantly to hurry from the room.

Without even troubling to lift his eyes from the paper this time, the King ordered, "Report back to the gate, Captain Lauder, and do not permit any of the Earl's retainers to enter with him."

"Sire!" With a brisk, military inclination of his head, Lauder strode rapidly after French Paris. Adam swallowed his astonishment at the quietly ruthless expression he had glimpsed on the King's face, and completed revising his estimate of the sixth Jamie. It was not fine clothes that went to make a King, he decided; nor a handsome face, nor strength of limb, nor yet all three together. It was something else, some quality of character he could not define, but King James was certainly possessed of it and Earl Bothwell would be either a very brave or a very stupid man if he defied it.

The audience chamber was very quiet now, for the whispering servants had withdrawn hastily at the stern dismissal of

French Paris, and Adam's attention wandered again until the silence was broken by the sound of the King's voice.

"Tell me," the King was leaning forward, folding the confession as he spoke, "why did you act as this confession says you acted?"

It was to himself the question was addressed, Adam realised with surprise, and stood tongue-tied, not knowing how to answer or how to address a King. Seton nudged him roughly and whispered,

"Speak up, fool! And call him 'Sire'."

"Sire, it was—it was for pity of Gilly," Adam stammered, "and for—for the saving of your life."

"My life, eh?" The King stroked his little red beard consideringly. "That is a strange answer, sirrah. The saving of my life would not benefit a clod like you with so much as another mouthful to eat or another inch of rag on your body. How then should it be your concern if witches plot to kill me?"

He was indeed shrewd, this young King, Adam acknowledged again. In that estimate at least he had not erred—but the question was still the very one he had himself asked Master Grahame, and so the answer to it was all ready on the tip of his tongue. Boldly he face the gaze of the heavy-lidded brown eyes.

"Sire," he told them, " 'tis the concern of every good subject in this land," and waited for some sign of pleasure in their gaze, but the King's expression did not alter. He spoke to the Chancellor instead, not taking his eyes off Adam's face, or turning his head.

"You hear that, Thirlestane? That is the voice of the common people of Scotland speaking. And you, who think too much of policy and not enough of people, would do well to heed it, and to remember that my title is not King of Scotland, but King of Scots. For these same common people have always loved their Stuart Kings.

"Did you know that, boy?" he asked Adam. "Did you know that when my mother, Queen Mary Stuart, was held at sword-point in this very palace by her rebellious nobles, it was the common people of Edinburgh who came to her rescue? Did you know that my grandfather, the fifth James of our name, used to roam the land in the guise of a beggar, making friends with the poorest of the poor among his people? Did you know that my great-grandfather, the fourth James, could out-run and out-wrestle any man in his kingdom, and that when he died a hero's death on Flodden battle-field the sorrow of Scotland moved even her enemies to tears?"

Adam choked down the lump that had unaccountably risen in his throat. "No, Sire," he confessed, "I did not know," and stared as if mesmerised into the brown eyes holding his own gaze.

"Then you must remember what I have said," the King told him gently, "for it is the King and people together who make our little nation, and so what you have done for me you have done also for all your brother-Scots.

"And now, witch!" His mood changing with a speed that shocked Adam out of his mesmerised state, the King turned to address Gilly. "What have you to say for yourself, eh?"

Adam felt Gilly jerk and stiffen in his grasp, saw the great plum-coloured bruises of her eyelids open slowly to show eyes dull with fatigue. Her voice came in a hoarse whisper.

"Nothing in—in my own defence, Sire, except that I acted from fear and not from malice towards you. And yet if—if the justice-fire must burn for those I betrayed through the pain of the torture . . ."

Her words faltered into silence for a moment, then finished almost inaudibly, "I beg of you to let me ask their pardon before I die in it also."

"You will have plenty of time to ask their pardon in Hell," the King told her roughly. "But meanwhile, answer my questions. This Devil you claim to have seen—was he a creature of the spirit, or a creature of flesh? Was he, in fact a demon in the shape of a man, or a man posturing as a demon?"

"He is a man, Sire," Gilly told him; faintly at first, and then with a rising note of hysteria in her voice. "A man like other men!"

"But not entirely like other men, eh?" the King pressed her. "For he plots my death, and—so you say—the Earl of Bothwell plots my death also. Therefore, answer me further, witch. Is this Devil the Earl of Bothwell, or is he not?"

If she answered straightforwardly with the true identity of the Devil, Adam realised, she would put Master Grahame in danger again, for there was still time for him to be arrested in mistake for his twin-brother. He hung on Gilly's answer, and drew a silent breath of relief when she said unsteadily,

"Sire, I—I have never seen the Earl of Bothwell."

"*Then look on him now, you lying vixen!*"

The voice rang out from the far end of the room, a powerful voice that came from a tall, powerfully-built young man pulling a plumed hat off bright, chestnut-coloured hair as he strode towards them. Grey-green eyes with odd little tawny flecks in them stared angrily down at Gilly's shrinking form, then turned to meet the King's gaze.

"To quote your own words, Sire—unless French Paris lies," Bothwell challenged the gaze, "'tis a very little witch to bring in evidence of so grave a charge against me."

Hands on hips, long legs straddled wide apart, he stood waiting the King's answer, and Adam could not help but compare the two men. Where the King was pale and flabby, he realised, Bothwell was brown and hard as teak; fiery where James was shrewd, arrogant where he was cautious. And handsome, Adam concluded, handsome as the devil; then thought what a foolish phrase that was.

"You have not made your duties to Us, my lord."

The King spoke quietly, with dignified use of the Royal pronoun, yet still he flinched at the wild glint that leapt suddenly in Bothwell's eyes. Startled, Adam thought, *He is afraid of Bothwell!* Then watching the King's expression as Bothwell dropped unwillingly to one knee before him, added to the thought, *And he hates the man.*

Bothwell looked up from his kneeling posture and spoke more calmly. "I crave your pardon, Sire, but French Paris told me that I am accused of conspiring with witches to kill you and seize your throne, and I was angered to know on what small evidence you have entertained such a monstrous charge."

King James studied him for a moment, his own features now also under control. "So you are innocent, Francis," he said at last, and with an impulsive gesture, Bothwell reached up to clasp one of the King's hands between his own.

"Jamie," he said softly. "Dear cousin! How could you

believe otherwise when you know that the greatest honour I could wish is to have my Prince so near a kinsman!"

"Yet you have come against me with drawn sword before this, Francis," the King reminded him. "With Ruthven and other rebellious nobles, as you must well remember."

"I was a youth, then—only eighteen years old," Bothwell protested, "and led astray by greybeards. I would not—"

"I was younger," the King interrupted sharply, "a mere lad of fifteen years: but that did not stop you or your companions from putting your swords to my throat! Do you remember what I said to you then, with your sword-point among those others?"

Bothwell looked down at their interclasped hands, not answering this, and in a voice charged suddenly with emotion the King said,

"We had played together as children, Francis, talked for long hours, walked with our arms around each other's necks; and I, who was so friendless and so frightened of the violent men around me, had thought you my friend. Look up, Francis, and hear me say again what I said to you that bitter day of swords."

Still Bothwell did not look up, and in the silence that followed, everyone in the room was sharply aware of the tensions between the two men. There was fear on the King's side, anger on Bothwell's, and hate in both of them. That had been clear in the first few seconds of their meeting. But now it was also clear that, on the King's side at least, there was the kind of admiring love a younger brother may feel for an older one; perhaps even something of the desperate desire a plain and lonely man may feel for the love of a handsome, popular friend.

For Adam, the moment held the shock of recognising in the King's emotion something of the feelings he had himself experienced and fought against so bitterly. Master Seton, he saw, was gaping spell-bound at this revelation of life in high places. Chancellor Thirlestane had retreated to a shadowed place behind the King's chair, and it was not possible to make out his expression. Tensely Adam waited the King's next words, and heard him say,

"I asked you then, *What has moved you, Francis, to take*

this course and come in arms against me? Have I ever done you any wrong, or given you cause for offence? I wish you a more quiet spirit, and that you may learn to live as a subject, otherwise you will fall in trouble."

Slowly, with easy grace, Bothwell rose upright and asked blandly, "And have I not lived as a subject?"

"You have continued a thorn in my flesh, and well you know it," the King snapped. "There was that business of the Spanish Letters, when you plotted with Philip of Spain to hold me prisoner while you invaded England. And—"

"It was not against you I plotted," Bothwell interrupted, "but against England. And I still hold to my reasons for that, for I will never approve the policy towards England that Chancellor Thirlestane has contrived for you."

". . . and now there is this occasion of witchcraft," the King over-rode his interruption, "which is a matter most foul, Francis, and hurtful to me."

Bothwell's eyes had quieted, but now the tawny flecks which seemed to signal anger with him, lit their grey-green colour again.

"Only because you choose to believe such a debased and infamous creature as this witch-woman here," he retorted. "Even although you yourself have said many times that the law of God is the only true touchstone of judgment, and God's law admits only witnesses which are famous and un-suspected. But even our municipal law condemns none with-out confession of the criminal or by a worthy court of his equals—"

"Then submit now to the law of the realm, which will give you no less justice!" the King cried. "I will raise a jury of your equals to try you, Francis. Give me your oath to go back quietly to your castle of Hermitage and I will—"

"A word with you, Sire."

Chancellor Thirlestane came quickly forward from his shadowed position and spoke low in the King's ear. "It would take too long for you to raise a jury of his peers, for he is too strongly entrenched in the nobility for any of them to volun-teer such service; and as a free man he will be a continuing danger to you. Persuade him to enter into ward in Edinburgh Castle *now*, Sire, and take action *now* against him."

Low as the Chancellor spoke, Bothwell appeared to have heard the words, for as soon as they were finished he hissed,

"You always were my enemy, Thirlestane, as I am yours; for I see you for what you are. *I* know why you have forced your English policy on the King, for I know your ambition. You see our King obtaining the English crown when Elizabeth dies, and you see yourself as Chancellor of both England and Scotland—the first man ever to hold so high an office. But I stand in the road of your ambition, and you know it. And so you would destroy me!"

Chancellor Thirlestane gave a menacing forward thrust of his heavy head. "And you, my lord," he growled, "you would destroy Scotland with your March-hare madness, your bristling wild-cat enmities. You have no more sense of discretion, my lord, than a bull charging a gate."

"Hold your tongues, both of you," James commanded sharply. "And you, Francis, take note that I am no child to be led by the nose by my Lord Chancellor or by anyone else. Lord Thirlestane is—"

"Is what, Jamie?" Bothwell roared his interruption. "Who *is* this 'Lord' Thirlestane that was only plain Sir John Maitland of Thirlestane until six months ago when he whined his way into the ranks of nobility? What is he compared to me, the fifth Earl of my line? A mushroom growth of a night beside a mighty cedar! Yet he would have me accused by debased persons that have desperately renounced their baptism; bereaved of land, life, and honour by the witness of poor beggars whose word, in any civil cause, would not prove the value of five shillings. And all without recourse to my legal entitlement of a jury of my peers! I shall not wait upon that, Sire. There is no 'Lord' Thirlestane will compass *my* death!"

Defiantly he raised his tall, feathered hat and clapped it on his head.

"Uncover, my lord," James commanded. "You are still in the presence of your King."

"My blood, Jamie," Bothwell retorted, "is as royal as your own!"

There was something frightening about his appearance now, Adam thought. He looked more than half-mad, in fact, with those tawny flecks glinting wildly in his eyes and the feathery plumes dancing crazily above them. The face he turned to Chancellor Thirlestane was a mask of snarling hate, but his voice had become almost purring as he said,

"I think myself beholden to you, Chancellor, that you do not wish me to be wearied by long process of law, but would persuade His Majesty to proceed summarily against me. Yet will I pay my debt to you in full, for you will never make this charge stick against me; and when I have proved it false —as prove it I will— I shall unseat you from your comfortable office. *And cut your throat for you!*"

With his voice rising to a roar again on the last words, Bothwell swung round and raced from the room; and carried away by the excitement of the moment, Master Seton shouted,

"Stop him! Stop him!"

No-one moved. There was no answering shout, no sudden stir from Lauder's men guarding the entrance to the Royal apartments. The King smiled a bitter little smile.

"There are five hundred Borderers ready to spring from the cobbles of Edinburgh's streets if Bothwell gives the word," he told Seton. "He must enter into the King's justice by his own consent, or not at all."

"Lord Chancellor!" Thirlestane came to stand at his elbow, and he continued, "I command you, my lord, raise the hue and cry instantly against every person named in this witch's confession. Prepare the Royal order summoning Bothwell into ward, and prepare also a warrant of outlawry against him. Hold this warrant ready to receive my seal if he refuses to give himself up to the summons."

"You must be able to make the charge against him stick, Sire," the Chancellor warned.

"I need no further advice about the Earl Bothwell," the King told him coldly. "The cards are all on the table between us now, and I shall play the game to win." He handed over Gilly's confession. "Now leave me, my lord. And you also, Master Seton. I wish private speech with these other two."

The Chancellor and Seton exchanged looks, the one offended, the other curious; then bowing, each unwillingly took his leave. Adam and the King were left staring at one another, for Gilly was so nearly unconscious by this time that she could hardly be said to be there.

"Now you have seen how little joy there is in kingship," the King said wearily after a moment. "But you, at least, have acted well in all this and I will see you rewarded—with land, if you are already a free man, with money to buy yourself free if you are bonded to Seton. Will that satisfy you?"

"No, Sire." With his heart in his mouth at the mere thought of such daring, Adam hurried to grasp the opportunity he had hoped for when he made his statement to the Town Council. "I ask only one reward of you. Let Gilly go free."

For a moment the King looked utterly taken aback, then angrily he asked, "Do you dare to jest, fellow? She is a confessed witch, forsworn to the Devil, and guilty of art and part in the highest crime in the land!"

"But Sire," Adam pleaded, "she was not forsworn of her own free will. Her mother did that for her when she was only a child, and she was forced to continue the company of witches for fear they would kill her if she refused. I am a witness to such threats. And she has done her best to mend all the harm in which she has been engaged—indeed, the plot against you would never have come to light if she had not been willing to tell me about it and seek my help in preventing it."

In his eagerness to plead Gilly's case, Adam had stepped forward, quite forgetting that she had been held upright by him throughout the long interview, and now before the King could answer him, she slid slowly down to the floor. Exclaiming in dismay, Adam whipped round to see her lying there, the napkin fallen from her head, her wounded hands lying slack beside her. The King cried out also, in disgust at the sight of her bloodied head, and said shudderingly as Adam knelt beside her,

"Cover up that head—cover it up! I have seen too much of blood already in my life."

She was alive, but only just, Adam realised. He replaced the napkin knowing he had to persuade the King *now* to save that little chance for life; but the King was still unnerved by sight of the blood, still muttering disjointedly of swords in the night, of violent men, and too much bloodshed in the land.

"I was three years old," came suddenly out of his muttering, "three years old, boy, when I first woke to the sight of a man's bearded face leaning over me and the feel of a sword against my throat. Do you understand that? I was Prince and pawn at the same time for the nobles of this kingdom—my father murdered, my mother a prisoner in England, and myself the football of power they kicked between them. Oh, it was a bloody game they played with their little King Jamie—a bloody game! And now I am sick of blood, sick at the very sight of it."

"Then save her!" Adam begged desperately. "For she, too, has suffered at the hands of bloody men, Sire, yet she is quiet, a gentle creature innocent of harm. The very beasts know that for they have no fear of her—even the wild hare yields to her touch. I have seen it."

"And horses?" With a spark of wistful interest returning to his eyes, the King added, "I love horses—and I ride well although my legs are weak for walking."

"Any animal, Sire," Adam assured him, and casting around for further inspiration remembered the Chancellor's warning, *You must be able to make the charge stick.* Eagerly he continued,

"And Sire, she could help you to make the charge against Bothwell stick, for you will remember that she was not given a proper chance to tell you the name of the man who posed as the Devil. But she does know it—I can swear to that—and once she is fit to speak again, she would tell it to you. Then, if you can make *that* man confess, you are certain to find the truth of Bothwell's part in the affair."

It was a safe enough offer to hold out as bait, he realised, looking down at Gilly's deathly-still face. It would be hours before she was fit to be questioned again—if she ever did recover consciousness; and by that time, Master Grahame would be well away on the tide as he had planned.

The King was looking indecisive now, fingering his beard, eyes wandering from one face to another. "Book of Exodus, Chapter 22, Verse 18," he said at last. "*Thou shalt not suffer a witch to live.* That is what Scripture has to say about witches, boy. You are asking me to go against God's Word."

"I am only asking you to show mercy!" Adam almost shouted in his despair. "I am only asking for the reward you offered me. I am only asking you to strike a bargain that will benefit yourself. Grant her, for God's sake, her life on any of these three counts."

There was a long silence in which Adam looked alternately from the King to Gilly, and incredibly at last, saw a slow flicker and opening of her bruised eyelids. She recognised him, and even made a painful attempt at a smile. He twisted his own face into what he hoped was a smile of encouragement, and nodded reassurance at her.

"I have decided," the King's voice said in the stillness. It came from close at hand, and Adam looked up, startled, to find him standing over himself and Gilly.

"I am a merciful man by nature," the King continued, "and so I want the least possible bloodshed over this affair. Therefore I have decided that this witch here must first identify all those who were ringleaders in the plot to murder me. Then, when I have succeeded in making a case against them that will ensure they are convicted of the crime of Treason by Witchcraft and will thus serve as evidence against Bothwell also, I shall allow her to go free and exact no other punishment from her.

"But lest even such an humble subject as you think me light in my decisions, note well that the bargain must stand in all particulars, and if even one guilty one escapes, it is void between us. This of Our Royal mercy, with Scriptural warrant, Matthew 5 and 7, *Blessed are the merciful, for they shall obtain mercy.*"

Adam gaped up at him, too overcome with relief and gratitude to realise the pomposity of the last sentence, and with no words to express his feelings, he seized the King's hand and kissed it. Jamie Sixth looked down with a peculiar sadness in his face.

"I wish," he said at length, "that more of my subjects would learn to show as much compassion for one another as you have had for this poor maiden. We would be a stronger nation so, and show a better face to the rest of the world."

"She needs a physician's care," Adam pointed out, seizing on this remark to dare fate for one last favour, but the King merely nodded and said,

"I shall send my own physician to her, then do you tell

your master he must find lodgings for you in Edinburgh, so that you can stay as long as I may need you."

He turned to walk away, and Adam watched him go, noting the scholar's stoop of his shoulders and his weak, shambling gait. As a man, he thought, the King did not cut much of a figure, but as a King...!

"You will live," he told Gilly, smiling down at her. "The King says so, and whatever others may think of him, he is truly a King."

Chapter 11

EXAMINATION OF WITCHES

In the ante-room to the Royal audience chamber, Adam stood shoulder to shoulder with Captain Dick Lauder, and stared through the open doorway between the two rooms.

The audience chamber was noisy with voices, and as crowded as it had been every day since the armed citizens of Edinburgh had ridden out on the hue and cry raised by the Chancellor, for the King had decided he would personally question all the scores of witches they had arrested. But now there was a new sound coming through the babble penetrating to the ante-room, and Adam frowned as he recognised the vibrant twanging of a jews' harp followed by a familiar, discordant chant,

Commer goe ye before, commer goe ye . . .

The King was making the witches sing for him. And yesterday he had commanded them perform the dance where they moved widdershins in an outward-facing circle––there was no end, it seemed, to his curiosity about their ritual! Adam made a small impatient sound, and glancing up to Captain Lauder wondered what thoughts lay behind the impassive face turned towards the din from the audience chamber.

Lauder, he had already decided, was more than just a handsome young soldier in a shining breast-plate and plumed helmet. Why otherwise should a captain of Royal guards trouble to make himself pleasant to the stable-boy who had been first on the scene with "the little witch", as they were calling Gilly now, when everyone else had forgotten his existence in the excitement of this spectacle the King was mounting? In the hope of picking up some scraps of information that these others would overlook, but which might just be useful to an ambitious man? Very likely so, Adam concluded, and let his glance at the captain grow to a hard, measuring gaze.

As if in response to the thoughts directed at him, Lauder turned to ask blandly, "And how does the King's latest ploy strike you, Adam?"

"'Tis a waste of time," Adam told him forcefully. "Dr. Fian and Mistress Sampson are the ringleaders of the plot, and he should be questioning them of playing games with this lesser sort of witch."

Lauder smiled like a man who knows more than he will say. "The Spanish Ambassador once called him the wisest fool in Christendom, Adam, and these are games with a purpose."

"But not the right purpose, surely," Adam argued. "Certainly I know the witches were all dumb with terror when they were first brought in, and all this dancing about and posturing has loosened their tongues. But giving them licence to perform like a band of mummers for the Court's pleasure will not help the King root out the truth of the plot."

"Ah-hah!" Lauder cocked a considering eye on him. "You are wrong there, Adam. And I could tell you why you are wrong if you would be frank with me on a certain matter."

Suspiciously Adam met the considering eye. "What matter?"

"The warlock, Richie Grahame." Lauder's expression was controlled again, but Adam guessed at the effort it was costing him not to sound eager. He looked away, thinking rapidly.

Gilly had obviously told the King the identity of the Devil, he reasoned, and Lauder had heard only enough about that to make him curious for more. So he had not been wrong in his estimate of *this* man! All the same, it was frustrating to be ignorant of what lay behind the scenes taking place in the audience chamber, and if the secret of the Devil was out anyway there would surely be no harm in trading information with Lauder. He looked back again, with his decision made.

"Very well. A bargain."

"Good! Now listen, for I may soon be needed in there." Lauder nodded towards the audience chamber. "There are more ringleaders to the plot than you have named, Adam. Another two of them are in there, in fact, at this moment; and they are among the ones who are still dumb—not with terror, but with defiance! But each statement the King coaxes from the foolish, bragging ones among the witches is being cross-checked with all the others. There is a great sifting process going on behind the foolery in there, and what remains when this sifting process is finished will be *evidence* —the clear, hard kind of evidence that will stand up strongly enough in court of law to convict all five ringleaders, and through them, the Earl of Bothwell. Now, about the warlock—"

A footstep behind him made him turn. Adam turned with him and saw Lord Chancellor Thirlestane enter the ante-room, a packet of papers in one hand and his bearded mouth set in a small, grim smile. Lauder swore under his breath at the interruption.

"Meet me after to-day's audience," he told Adam rapidly, then moved towards the Chancellor and nodded at the papers in his hand.

"So you found them, my lord."

"And they are proof positive!" The Chancellor tapped the papers triumphantly.

"Good! Now we will have action."

With a nod of satisfaction, Lauder fell into step with the Chancellor as he continued towards the door of the audience chamber, and Adam moved quickly to close in behind them. As he had guessed would happen, the press of Palace servants and courtiers beyond the doorway made room respectfully for the Lord Chancellor's entry. The witches crowding the centre of the floor also made way for him to approach the King's chair, and Adam had no difficulty in placing himself at the forefront of the mob of spectators. The King took the packet of papers from the hand of the Chancellor, and immediately his glance travelled to two of the women witch-prisoners. Quickly, then, he opened the packet and began reading.

Adam stared at the two women the King's gaze had singled out, and saw that one of them was young and very beautiful. The other was twice her companion's age, with a face that had a great look of command about it, and both were very well-dressed in comparison with the rest of the witches. Indeed, Adam thought, if they had not been herded along with the other prisoners he would have assumed them to belong to the group of Court ladies among the spectators. His gaze roamed from them, seeking Gilly, and found her near the King's chair.

She was standing very still, bandaged hands folded in front of her, eyes downcast. The napkin she still wore around her wounded head was filthy with three nights hard lying in the Tolbooth jail, but she was not as pale as she had been, and there was a look about her—almost of peace, Adam thought, searching for words to identify the sense of repose that came from her still figure. He waited for her to glance up so that he could signal encouragement with a look or a nod, but her gaze remained directed down at the splints in which her broken thumbs had been set, and he looked around among the other prisoners.

Dr. Fian was there, he noted: spare and erect as ever and still neat in spite of his time in prison, his cold grey gaze fixed on some distant point that ignored the restless throng of prisoners and spectators. He was standing a little aloof from the rest of the witches—or perhaps it was they who were keeping their distance from him. Perhaps, Adam thought, they were still afraid of him, and shivered a little in spite of himself as his gaze travelled on in search of Agnes Sampson.

She was nowhere to be seen, however, and now it seemed the King had read enough of the papers in his hand. He was looking up from them, his gaze once more on the two well-dressed women. The Lord Chancellor muttered something to him. He nodded, then called,

"Mistress Euphemia McCalzean!"

The woman with the commanding face glanced grimly at her companion then swept forward to make a formal curtsy to him.

"Mistress Barbara Napier!"

A look of panic flashed over the younger woman's face as the King called her also, but she recovered herself quickly and came forward to curtsy as Mistress McCalzean had done. The King regarded them soberly, then addressed himself to Mistress McCalzean.

"This is strange company, mistress, for a daughter of Lord Cliftonhall!"

His gaze travelled to Mistress Napier. "And for a lady of

such illustrious family as the Napiers of Merchiston."

"We have been falsely arrested," Mistress McCalzean snapped.

"Indeed?" The King held up the papers for her to see. "These letters to you from the Earl of Bothwell tell a different story. And the little *billets-doux* he has written to Mistress Napier here, speak of other things than love."

Mistress Napier flushed brick-red, and with a gasp of rage Mistress McCalzean shrilled, "I demand to speak to my man of law, Sire. 'Tis no justice to ransack our private papers thus while we are held in prison with this peasant rabble."

"You will have justice enough," the King told her grimly. "Wait you, till you hear what Sir James Melville has to say."

Turning, he gestured sharply to an elderly man standing nearby with a sheaf of documents in his hands. "Read, Melville," he commanded. "Read from the affidavit sworn by the man-witch, Jockie Greymeill."

"Sire!" The elderly man shuffled through his documents, muttered a few lines from one of them, and then read aloud: *"Then some that were in the church were very insistent to have the image, and Naip cried out loud, 'Where is the image that he promised us?' And Cane also cried, 'When is the King to burn?' And for that I thanked God the King's health was good, Rob the Rowar did give me a sore buffet on the face, and then—"*

"That is enough." Curtly the King brought the reading to an end and leaned back in his chair observing the two women. They had both gone very pale, Adam saw, and the young one was trembling. Captain Lauder had moved to stand directly behind them, and they seemed uneasily aware of his presence towering over them.

"I have now collected half a hundred statements about the witches 'Cane' and 'Naip'," the King remarked at length. He looked at Gilly. "Name these two for me," he commanded. "Mistress McCalzean first. Who is she?"

"Cane." Gilly spoke softly but clearly.

"And Mistress Napier?"

"Naip."

"Lies, lies!" Mistress McCalzean burst out furiously. "I demand an end to it, Sire. I will not stand here and be forced to take part in this debased game you have invented for the amusement of the Court!"

"You have not been forced to take part in anything yet," the King told her tartly. "But now you will be so forced, mistress, and 'tis not myself who will see to that; for now we have reached the part in the game which comes just before the torture of the rope and is called *Examination of the prisoners for witch-marks.*"

"No!" As one woman Mistress McCalzean and Mistress Napier jerked out their protest, and Mistress McCalzean added in a shaking voice, "I was acquainted with your Royal mother, Sire, and she would not have allowed the common executioner to touch the sleeve of ladies of our standing, far less search their persons with his filthy hands."

"You do well to quote my Royal mother," the King retorted venomously, "for she also knew all about murder! But I am not so nice in my manners as she was, and so I do not intend to lose my throne to a Bothwell—as she did! These are matters you should have pondered, mistress, before you dabbled in witchcraft; and more especially before you recommended Earl Bothwell to the services of the warlock, Richie Grahame."

Adam glanced swiftly around in search of reactions to this mention of Richard Grahame—the first in all the three long days of the King's interrogation of the witches. Fian was as aloof as ever, he saw, although the rest of the prisoners were buzzing with excited questioning. He caught Gilly's eye at last and saw her nod slightly as if answering the question in his raised eyebrows. She *had* named Richard Grahame as the Devil, he decided, then found his attention jerked back to Mistress McCalzean.

She was backing away from the King's chair, gathering the stiff folds of her brocaded gown around her as she screamed,

"The common hangman shall not touch *my* person, Jamie Stuart! I carry a witch-mark—I admit that freely, and I demand a jury trial within the High Court of Justiciary on any charge you may bring against me."

"And I!" Mistress Napier chimed in, her sullen eyes now sparking watchful hostility at the King. "The Napiers have powerful friends among the merchant guilds of Edinburgh, Sire, as your Treasury may find to its cost if you proceed summarily against one of my name."

The King smiled the satisfied smile of a man who has just played a winning hand at cards. Formally he said,

"We grant of Our Royal justice your request for a trial in the High Court of Justiciary, on the charge of Treason by Witchcraft."

His eyes travelled over the heads of the two women, to Captain Dick Lauder. "And I command you, Captain, escort these Our subjects back to their prison and give the Governor of the Tolbooth Our order that they may purchase comforts to suit their rank. Inform the Governor also that he may permit any gentleman of the law or the church to visit them freely; but that on pain of death to himself, he is to allow no other visitors and to keep the prisoners strait until the day of trial."

"Sire!" Lauder gave his stiff, military bow and touched both women on the shoulder. They followed him tamely enough as he cleared a passage-way for their exit, but at the door of the audience chamber Mistress McCalzean turned to shout,

"I warn you, Jamie Stuart, I shall fight for my life! And if I win, a better man than you will sit in judgment here— a proper man, and not the snuffling, Bible-thumping pedant that you are!"

"Do not deceive yourself, mistress," the King called back. "You will lose your case, and you will be burned—alive!"

There was a gasp from his hearers at this last word, and even Mistress McCalzean's defiance was visibly shaken before she finally disappeared, but Adam was too busy reckoning up the score to pay full attention to the exchange. "Five ring-leaders," Lauder had said, which left only Sampson, Fian, and Richard Grahame to be accounted for; and if the King could gather enough evidence for a successful trial against these three also, he would have the case he needed to present against the Earl of Bothwell.

But Richard Grahame was still at large, and so the King might still fail in his purpose, for the evidence of all five ring-leaders was interlocking. Which meant that Bothwell might still go free, and Gilly ... What *would* the King do about Gilly then? What would he do about all the witches? He was laughing at them again, poking fun at the ritual some of them had described in their confessions, demanding to know what the Devil looked like. The witches began to answer all at once, in a clamour of voices.

... like a beast with horns ... a nose falling down sharp like an eagle's beak ... a long black gown on him and wings, and a beast-head above it ... claws ... his touch cold and hard, like iron ... speaks rough and ghost-like ... eyes like red coals, and rips with his claws ...

The clamouring voices rose in crescendo, and the King's laughter rose with them, deliberately provoking them to further excess.

"Liars!" he shouted, and teased them again. "You dreamed it all. You are nothing but a pack of liars!"

"We are not all liars!"

The words came in a shriek from the door of the audience chamber, a shriek so dreadful that it froze the noise in the room as instantly as death would have done. And like some wild apparition of Death itself standing there, with the black-hooded figures of the executioner and his assistant on either side of her, Agnes Sampson surveyed the faces turning slowly towards her presence.

Her clothes were dishevelled, the once-neat ruff round her neck torn to shreds, her gown unlaced with the skirt sitting at an awkward angle to the bodice. Her glaring face was mottled a peculiar blue-white. Her cropped head, with the line of the knotted rope traced in a wide, bloody band around it, shook like the head of a woman stricken with palsy.

She opened her mouth again, and the sound that came from it was a snarl. Saliva dribbled from the corners of her open mouth, and she lunged forward, carrying executioner and assistant with her in the fury of her sudden rush towards the King's chair. He flinched back from her, but the soldiers on guard at either side of his chair thrust their pikes forward to cross protectively in front of him, and the men holding her jerked her to a halt. The executioner clapped his hand over her mouth to stifle the shout breaking from it, and called out breathlessly,

"Sire, she has confessed! The pain broke her, and the Clerk

to the Privy Council has got all of her confession in writing, and I—"

The breathless voice broke off in a howl of pain as Agnes Sampson bit into the fingers over her mouth. The executioner whipped his bloodied fingers away, and speech came rushing from her.

"I am no liar—I have no need to lie like these other fools, for I am a true witch with power to heal and power to curse and a spirit in my keeping to do my bidding and prophesy for me. And that is why that proud-faced besom, Cane, sent Earl Bothwell to *me* for help in his purpose in the first place. *Read me the King's horoscope, Wise Wife,* he asked of me, but this I would not do, knowing well it was treason, and laughed in his face. And so he scorned me, yet lived to regret it—as you shall regret your scorn of me now, Jamie Stuart —for I called up the spirit in my keeping in the shape of a great black dog, and caused it speak to him with the voice of the dead, and did read a prophecy for him; which was that he should kill his Sovereign or his Sovereign should kill him. And so he was hasty to make it a good outcome for himself, and would have the covens kill you for him. In the doing of which I proved my power also, for no-one that lives shall mock that power; and so it was *I* who made the image that would burn, with a swallow's heart thrust into one side and a swallow's liver into the other; and it was—"

She looked mad—she *was* mad, Adam thought, feeling a chill up his spine as her voice raved on and on; mad enough at least to fire her own funeral pyre with this wild boasting of witch-power: then realised with dismay what this meant. The King could not bring a mad-woman to trial. She *had* to be speaking the truth or all her raving against Bothwell would be useless as evidence.

The King was trying to stem the flow of her words, shouting at her, beating his fist on the arm of his chair; but it took the executioner's arm locked suddenly round her neck from behind to choke the raving into quiet. The King leaned forward, scarlet in the face with exertion, his hands shaking where they rested on the arms of his chair.

"Prove it!" he challenged her. "Give me one single proof of the power you claim, and I will believe you are not a liar like these other mountebank fools!"

Slowly, at a nod from him, the executioner released his hold on Agnes Sampson. She stood panting for several moments, then gradually as her breathing eased her face settled into lines of quiet, almost sleepy cunning. When she spoke at last, it was softly, with a strange coaxing gentleness in her voice.

"A word in your ear, Sire; a private word."

The colour drained suddenly from the King's face. He looked at the pike-blades still guarding him, from these to the warning face of his Lord Chancellor, then to the elderly, worried face of Secretary Melville. Neither of them spoke, but their very silence counselled caution more strongly than words could have done. The King's gaze travelled round the faces of the prisoners, shifted to those of the spectators.

He was a very frightened man, Adam guessed. But he was also King, and all these people were his subjects. How could he act the craven before them? Yet how could a man who was sickened by the very sight of blood allow that fearful, bloodied head close enough to whisper in his private ear?

"Release her!" The King's voice came harshly, and the black-masked figures dropped their hold on Agnes Sampson.

"Raise your pikes," he ordered the soldiers, and reluctantly they returned their guarding blades to an upright position.

The King rose to his feet. "Back, all of you." With both hands he gestured prisoners and spectators alike to the furthest limits of the room, and they crowded back on one another leaving Agnes Sampson standing erect and alone at its centre. The King stepped down from his chair-dais and walked towards her.

Slowly and steadily he walked, and steadily she watched him with that expression of sleepy cunning on her bloated face. They stood face to face, their bodies almost touching, then, "Speak, witch!" he commanded, and bent his head so that she could whisper into his ear.

She was taller than he, so that the gesture resembled that of a man bending to lay his head on the executioner's block; and at the sight of it and the unprotected neck it exposed, a low murmur of horror went through the watching crowd. Adam felt the same sound come involuntarily to his own lips, and watched tensely the slow inclination of the witch's bloated face to the waiting, listening ear.

She whispered, paused, whispered again, then raised her head to give a sudden peal of triumphant, hysterical laughter. The King looked up at her, a dazed expression on his face, then like a man in a dream he walked slowly back to his chair. The executioner and his assistant came forward to resume their grip on Agnes Sampson, but although her laughter ceased at their touch, the watching crowd stayed crammed fearfully as far away from her as they could. Once again the King surveyed their faces, then he said quietly,

"She does not speak out of madness, for she has the power she claims. This she has proved by the words she has just spoken to me, for until this moment, these held a secret which was known to only two people in the world—my Queen and myself. This is witchcraft, and so now I do truly believe her guilty of treason by witchcraft, and that she is fit to be tried for this in open court. Master Executioner, do you hand her over now to the Palace guard to be conveyed to the Tolbooth prison and kept straitly there, and then proceed forthwith to the questioning of the prisoner, Doctor John Fian."

Fian! Fian! Fian! The name ran in a whisper round the crowd, and a flurry of movement took place in the audience chamber—a tramp of feet from guards marching to take charge of Agnes Sampson, a surge among the crowd, shouts, and a single, protesting voice as Fian was heaved forth from among them. The executioner seized him, pinning his arms behind his back, and Adam had one brief glimpse of his face, set hard with determination as he and Agnes Sampson were hustled from the room. The crowd surged and eddied back to former positions, and the King resumed his seat. The Lord Chancellor bent towards him.

"'Tis late, and you have accomplished much, Sire," he pointed out. "Will you not rest this matter till to-morrow?"

"No, my lord." Stubbornly the King shook his head. "I must see first how this Fian bears up under the questioning."

"He looked determined. You may have long to wait," the Chancellor warned, and with a start Adam realised how dark it had grown in the audience chamber.

"Bring candles!" he heard the order shouted, and shifted

from one aching foot to the other, the very thought of candles adding to the heat in that already stuffy room bringing the sweat out on him. But, he told himself, if that pale and spindle-shanked young man in the Royal chair could continue this test of endurance, then so could he—even if Fian lasted the night out under questioning.

But Fian did not last the night out. It was only just over an hour later when he was brought back to the audience chamber, and already sleepy in the overcrowded warmth of the room, Adam missed his entrance completely.

The first he knew of it was the voice of the King himself crying out on a high note of horror,

"Cover him up! Cover him up for God's sake, and bring a stool for him to sit on!"

Struggling to the edge of the crowd that hemmed him in, Adam saw Secretary Melville hastily snatch at a kerchief offered him and drop it over Fian's hands. Someone else was passing a stool over the heads of the crowd, and the master executioner pushed Fian down on to it. His covered hands rested limply on his knees, and almost immediately, blood began to soak through the kerchief over them. A thicker one was called for, and hastily produced. Without prompting, then, Fian began to talk.

For another hour he spoke steadily, in a slow, monotonous voice that allowed time for every word to be written down; then the steady dictation began to falter, and he slumped on his stool, drooping lower and lower with fatigue. He was a sorry-looking object now, Adam thought, surprised to find even himself pitying Fian at last, and was relieved eventually to hear the King announce that the rest of the confession would be heard on the following day.

It was not until he was out in the reviving air outside the Palace, however, that Adam realised how little of hard fact there had been in Fian's long, monotonous dictation. True he had talked about witchcraft, but only about witchcraft in general. He had not even touched upon the facts of the plot against the King, or mentioned one single incriminating circumstance against himself or against Richard Grahame.

Suspiciously Adam stared after the dark procession of prisoners disappearing in the direction of the Tolbooth; then, with a sinking feeling at his heart, he set off to his lodgings to have some supper before he kept the appointment he had arranged as he waited in the ante-room with Captain Lauder.

Chapter 12

THE DEVIL HIS DUE

The lanternlight in the Palace gate-house was nicely shadowed and Adam sat well back in the dim corner he had chosen for himself. It was proving unexpectedly easy to talk to Captain Lauder, he thought, and now that he had taken the plunge, it was a considerable relief to tell someone his secret knowledge of Grahame the alchemist and Grahame the warlock.

He talked steadily on, his physical eye on the fair, handsome head bent forward to listen intently, but his mind's eye filled with the figures of the dark legion gathered at the Hallowe'en Sabbat. Lauder made no comment at all, although he looked up sharply at the tremble that crept involuntarily into Adam's voice when he described the waylaying of the Devil on the road to North Berwick; and at the end of the story he sat back in thoughtful silence, chin on chest and eyes closely studying the long booted legs thrust out before him.

"And this alchemist fellow you spoke of," he remarked eventually, "I suppose you have checked that he took ship as planned?"

"Aye." Adam nodded in the direction of Leith, the port of Edinburgh. "I asked at the shipping office down there in Leith, and a clerk told me a fishing-boat from Prestonpans had transferred him to the berth he had booked on the barque *Horizon*, outward bound for France."

"Have you ever thought, young Adam—" the fair head lifted and eyes gleamed with reflected light from the lantern, "—of taking up a soldier's life?"

"A soldier's life?" Adam stared for a moment, then laughed without mirth in his voice. "I am a bond-servant. My master owns my labour until I am twenty-four years old, and—"

Lauder interrupted, "The King would buy you free. You

have done his cause great service." He stood up, stretching himself tall in the small guard-room. "A man can rise far in my profession. Look at me! I was a barefoot lad like yourself once, but a sharp mind and a little courage have worked wonders for me. And shall work more, I warrant you, or my name is not Dick Lauder."

He strolled to the door and stood listening to the tramp of the sentries at the gate. Over his shoulder he added, "You have that sharpness of mind too, and the alchemist has trained it well. Moreover, you have shown a fair degree of courage in this affair. And you know how to be ruthless in your own interests. That last was a lesson I too had to learn before I could climb from the state you are in now."

Adam stared at the head outlined against the starry darkness outside the door, and wondered at the confidences the dim lantern-light had bred. Lauder the dashing soldier, Lauder the smart young officer of the Palace guards—a barefoot lad like himself, hungry sometimes, maybe dodging blows, despised, bullied. It was hard to believe! But did he want to be as Lauder was now—hard, climbing, ruthless? Did he want the eyes of others to measure him as his own eyes had measured Lauder in the ante-room that morning? Abruptly he said,

"I have no taste for soldiering. And so I gain Gilly's life, I will have reward enough."

"A pity." Lauder, shrugged, turning his head away. "I would have used my influence on your behalf."

He stepped down from the doorway, and Adam rose to follow him as he made for the Palace gates. The street of Canongate lay beyond the gates, stretching dark and silent up to the wall surrounding the city of Edinburgh itself, and gazing up its length Adam said quietly,

"'Tis not my business to ask why you wanted all this information about Richie Grahame, sir, but it does concern me to know where he is now. He is the last of the ringleaders untaken, after all, and the most important of them."

Lauder laughed shortly. "Do you think I would be standing here if I knew where to lay hands on him? It would mean promotion for me if I could do that, and it was from your story I hoped to gather the necessary clue."

Adam felt the greasy pie his landlord had given him for supper move uneasily in his stomach. Richard Grahame still at large, and Dr. Fian playing for time in his confession—the affair was far from finished yet, he thought despondently, then was startled by the sudden sight of lights moving at the head of the Canongate and the sound of running feet somewhere in the darkness. He gripped Lauder's arm, remembering the determination on Fian's face as he was dragged out for questioning, and exclaimed,

"Something has happened about Fian!"

Lauder shook him off. "Fian is safe behind walls six foot thick," he snapped. "Now be quiet and let me listen to—"

"I feel it in my bones," Adam interrupted. "Fian is dead, or escaped, or—or—"

Fiercely Lauder rounded on him. "If Fian has escaped I will let you ride with me yourself to take him again. That is how certain I am you are wrong. I saw him locked into his cell, I tell you—locked and double-locked. Now get back to your lodgings—away from here! Go on!"

"No!" Adam backed, defying him. The lights were almost on them now, the running feet were materialising into men pounding down the Canongate, shouting hoarsely as they ran. Lauder whirled to snap out orders to the sentries, and one of them went haring off towards the Palace while the others closed up behind him, pikes advanced. Lauder's sword came whistling from its sheath, then the men were on them, lanterns wildly waving, open mouths shouting alarm. Lauder caught the leading one by the neck of his doublet and shook him brutally.

"Now!" he snarled. "Speak brief and to the point."

"Fian—the warlock—escaped!" The man gasped out the words, half-choked by Lauder's hold on him, and the babbling of the others rose even louder.

"Quiet!" A parade-ground roar from Lauder hushed them suddenly. He released his hold on their leader, and sullenly feeling his bruised throat the man added,

"He tempted the turnkey to drink wine with him, drugged his drink, and stole his keys."

"How long ago?"

The man spread his hands helplessly. "Who knows? Hours

maybe. The turnkey is still in a deep stupor."

Lauder stood frowning for a moment, then suddenly sheathed his blade again and started to rap out orders to the citizens crowding around him.

"You—rouse the Lord Provost, and give my warrant to raise the hue and cry. You—rouse the Dean of Guild and charge him bring out the craftsmen flying their banner of the Blue Blanket, every man armed with the tools of his own craft. You—wake the bell-ringer at Saint Giles and tell him sound the peal for all the other church bells to ring. No citizen must sleep this night, no corner of the city be left unsearched. And so hurry, all of you."

A sharp clop and rattle of hooves sounded from behind him, and swinging round towards the troop of horses advancing from the forecourt of the Palace, he told one of his pike-men,

"Run fast to the Lord Chancellor with the news. Tell him I have roused the city, and am now deploying horsemen to spread the alarm to all points of the compass."

"Sir—Captain Lauder—!" As the soldier ran off with his pike at the trail, Adam thrust forward, shouting, through the dispersing group of citizens.

"Let me go with you! You promised—you said I could ride with you if Fian escaped."

The troop was bearing down on them, thundering to a halt. Lauder reached for the rein of the horse his messenger-sentry had fetched for him and swung up into the saddle, but Adam jumped to clutch at the horse's mane.

"Stand back!" Lauder roared, and struck down at him.

"You promised!" Adam yelled, and hung grimly on, ignoring the sting of the cheek cut by Lauder's knuckles. "*And I know where Fian is!*"

The tossing head he gripped was abruptly still as Lauder reined hard on it. Adam's glance strained upwards. The angry face bent towards him said softly,

"I will give you the beating of your life if you are lying."

"And be disgraced if you do not believe me!" Adam retorted.

Lauder straightened in the saddle and snapped out to the rider beside him, "Sergeant, take over another mount and give yours to this fellow."

"Sir?" Astonished and resentful the sergeant hesitated.

"Quickly!" Lauder roared. The sergeant slid from his saddle. The trooper beside him did likewise. Adam ran quickly to mount the sergeant's horse as he took over the trooper's mount, and yelled to Lauder,

"Eastwards through the King's Park. Through Duddingston village, and keep bearing east."

He wheeled his mount to the left of the troop, and heard Lauder shouting to him to lead on as he kicked heels hard into its flanks. The beast leaped forward, then Lauder's mount drew up on him and they were riding neck and neck with shouted question and answer passing between them and the troop thundering close behind through the darkness of the great wooded hunting-park lying east of the Palace.

The village of Duddingston dropped behind them with no slackening of their pace. Lauder was literally giving him his head, Adam realised, and felt a second of panic in case he had dared too much. But the flash of inspiration that had come to him could not have been a false one, he argued. All he knew of Fian fitted too well with it.

The great black book of his office as Registrar to the Devil —that was the key to the reason for his escape! Had not Gilly said that all the doings of the witches were written down in it? And had not he, himself, heard the Devil calling the roll from it at the Sabbat of Hallowe'en? The book held all the secrets of the covens. And that was why Fian had yielded so quickly to the torture. That was why he had pretended to confess, then feigned a greater exhaustion than he really felt—so that he could win time to escape: *time to return to Tranent to destroy the black book!*

The troop galloped through the village of Niddry. Beyond that lay Wallyford, and only a mile or so further on, Tranent itself. Adam glanced at the hard profile keeping company with him, guessing at the reason for Lauder's continued silence. Lauder did not dare to doubt the success of their mission, he decided, for to do so meant admitting that the bright young captain of guards could be toppled from the position he had fought for so ruthlessly. Lauder was afraid; but *he* was not afraid for himself. He was only afraid for Gilly, and surely that made him the stronger character of the two? The alchemist had been right when he said, *Compassion is not a weakness; it is a strength*. He called sharply hearing a new note of confidence, even of authority, in his own voice,

"Slow your troop, Captain. We are nearly there."

Lauder raised a hand high, and followed Adam's example of slowing his horse's pace to a canter. They were passing the grove of beeches around the alchemist's house, and for a moment it seemed to Adam that he saw a line of light through the trees. But the alchemist had fled abroad, he reminded himself. He must have imagined that glimpse of light. He turned his head to speak to Lauder.

"The fourth house after we pass this scatter of houses outside the village itself; the house with its gable-end to the street and a fleur-de-lis at the peak of the gable."

"You had better be right." The ominous ring in Lauder's voice covered an even deeper apprehension than he had guessed at, Adam realised, and he answered curtly,

"I know what I am doing."

He pointed ahead, ignoring the jerk of surprise Lauder gave at his tone. "There, on the left—that white-washed gable."

"And you think he is inside there?"

"I *know* he is."

"Pull up, then." Lauder gave the signal for a halt, and pulled up his own mount. Adam slid down beside him as he dismounted, and the rest of the troop left their mounts to come clustering around them. Quietly Lauder gave them instructions for surrounding Fian's house, then led them, cat-like, along the fifty yards that separated it from their halting-place. The pike-man he had detailed to follow himself and Adam was close on their heels as they came to a silent halt at the foot of the flight of stone steps set parallel to the front of the house and leading up to its front door.

Like prowling shadows, the rest of the troopers dispersed around the house. Adam glimpsed a faint light moving behind one of the windows in line with the doorway above him, and nodded as Lauder whispered the same discovery. Lauder stepped back, motioning Adam with him.

"Now!" he whispered, and the pike-man charged up the

steps, aiming his weapon at the door. Its point penetrated just above the lock, and the wood cracked under the forceful thrust of the long, heavy blade. Bounding up the steps on the pike-man's heels, Lauder charged his shoulder at the cracking door, and both men ducked swiftly back to allow Adam room for the third and final charge that burst the lock free from the wood splintering around it. The door swung open, and they saw Fian.

A solitary candle in a holder on the mantelpiece lit him as he knelt staring towards them, a tinder-box held awkwardly in hands crusted with dried blood; and scattered all around him were the pages of his black book of office, ripped out and ready for burning. Lauder would have rushed forward to seize him, but Adam was a pace ahead of him and the pike-man, and he barred their road with arms outstretched across the door-way. There was something strange about Dr. Fian, he realised —an unnatural fixed stare about his eyes that made it look as if he had not grasped the danger their coming meant to him. Almost instantly, it seemed, Lauder realised this also, for he did not push against Adam's restraining arm. All three in the doorway waited, regarding the kneeling figure curi-ously, and Dr. Fian spoke at last.

"Once more, ere thou die, thou shalt be mine."

The words came in a tranced ghostly whisper of his own voice. The pike-man exclaimed under his breath, and Adam felt the pressure of his body removed as he backed away from the door. Lauder's arm trembled against his own, and Lauder's voice also trembled as he whispered,

"Speak to him! Find out what he means!"

Adam's mind raced. Fian was quoting someone else's words, he guessed. That was the only thing which could make sense of what he had said. But whose words? Whose power held Fian in this spell-bound condition? And how could he break through to the tranced mind that held the answers to such questions? He licked his dry lips and carefully shaped an idea into speech.

"The Devil is gone back into hell, John Fian. He cannot speak to you now."

Dr. Fian blinked. His fixed stare faltered, and a look of frightened cunning crept into it. He peered towards Adam.

"You are lying. He spoke to me in jail, in a—in—in a dream..."

His voice trailed away, then grew stronger. "Yes, I had a dream, a strange dream when he spoke to me and told me how to escape and what I must do. And he was waiting here when I arrived, and that is what he said. *Once more ere thou die, thou shalt be mine.* And I am his. I am forsworn to the Devil, and so I must do as he bid me."

His hands came together, striking steel off flint; and as the spark leapt out to fall on the topmost page Lauder shouted, springing forward and knocking Adam aside as he sprang. He seized Fian, and at his touch, the last of the schoolmaster's trance fell away from him. Wriggling violently he slipped from Lauder's grasp and bounded to the far side of the room. The pike-man at the door whistled shrilly. Lauder drew his sword, and, cautiously stalking, drove Fian into a corner of the room.

Fian backed against the wall there, then jerking his head forward spat at Lauder. "*That* for your sword, Captain," he said contemptuously. "Kill me! Kill me now, for it will not avail you to keep me alive."

There were feet running outside the house, pounding up the steps leading to the door. Fian shouted above the noise,

"I shall not talk! I shall never confess a word, though they break every bone in my body with torture!"

The soldiers pounding up the steps burst into the room. "Seize him!" Lauder called. "Take him outside."

They rushed him in a pack, and Lauder called his sergeant back as Fian was carried outside.

"Gather up these pages, sergeant," he instructed, "and be careful not to miss any. The King will not need a confession from Fian so long as he has these. Then tear this house apart for every written scrap of paper you can find."

"Sir!" the sergeant knelt to begin gathering up the pages of Fian's black book, and Adam at last succeeded in getting the attention he had been vainly trying to attract from Lauder.

"You have been wasting time—are wasting it now," he said urgently. "*He was waiting here when I arrived*—that was what Fian said, and 'he' means Richie Grahame. Do you not see? The Devil bade him burn the book, and Richie Grahame is the Devil."

"My God!" Lauder stared around wildly. "You mean—?"

"No—not here in this house." Adam was already rushing for the door and he threw the words over his shoulder as he ran. "But he has not gone far; he cannot have gone far in the time available. And I think I know where he is!"

Lauder was at his heels as he clattered down the stone steps outside, Lauder bellowing a string of troopers' names and mouthing rapid instructions as they came running towards him. Adam raced ahead to mount his horse, but Lauder and his men were only seconds behind him as he swung into the saddle.

"The beech-grove on the right, just beyond the village," Adam yelled, and heeled his mount forward with Lauder and some twenty of his men following hard behind.

They were there within a few minutes, the whole troop sweating and panting as they halted at the signal Lauder relayed from Adam, and slid down to join them in the shelter of the trees.

"There! D'ye see?" Adam gripped Lauder's shoulder and pointed to a line of light glimmering faintly between the trees —the light he had dismissed earlier as something in his own imagination. "He is hiding there—in his brother's house. And what better place to hide than in the house of a recluse that *no-one* ever visits!"

"You used to visit him," Lauder said, staring at the light, and quickly Adam answered,

"Aye, but secretly! Not a soul in the village knew I did so—far less Richie Grahame."

"Dispositions?" Lauder asked.

"One door in the wall facing us now, and one window facing the door," Adam told him. "Concentrate your men at these points, and you cannot fail to take him."

"Good lad!" Lauder turned to move among his men, giving them quick, quiet instructions. One half of the party split off from the rest, and began casting in a wide arc through the trees. Lauder held the others steady till his advance party began closing their arc towards the back of the alchemist's house, then he signalled the other men forward.

They moved singly, dodging from the cover of one tree-trunk to another, and only the scuffling sound of their feet in the grass betrayed their progress. Adam rejoined Lauder as he crouched behind the tree nearest the house, and together they eyed the line of light down one side of the door.

"'Tis an old door, and loose, to show the light like that," Lauder muttered, and Adam whispered in reply,

"One good charge will break it open."

Lauder nodded, and turned to beckon. A burly trooper emerged from behind the tree next in line to their own. Lauder whispered to him, then without warning, both men charged the door. Adam was on their heels instantly, and behind him he heard the rush and scurry of the rest of the troop. The door burst wide open under the impact of the two charging men. Light flowed out among the trees. There was yelling, the clashing of steel and a loud sound of breaking glass, then Adam found himself blundering to a halt in the alchemist's work-shop with troopers all round him, and thick green glass showering down as the troopers at the window finished breaking through it with their pikes.

Every candle in the work-shop was lit, he realised, and the place was over-poweringly warm. Then he saw the black-gowned figure turning at bay in front of the tall furnace at the far end of the work-shop, and his heart tripped suffocatingly.

Master Grahame! his senses cried in alarm; but his brain answered calmly, "Richard Grahame, the warlock," for Master Grahame was safely on his way to France and the black-gowned figure was advancing the red-hot point of the long iron poker he held in one hand, and yelling fiercely,

"Back! Back, soldier-scum, before I conjure you with my magic!"

They hesitated in face of the threat—even Lauder hesitated, and grinning, the warlock moved crab-wise, touching a draughter open at the foot of the furnace as he moved. The furnace doors were open, and as he moved away from them the flames within leapt redly into view and the in-suck of air through the draughter caused something to rise at the heart of the fire—a face, a grinning beast-face over-topped with wings blazing scarlet flames.

"The Devil!" One voice from among the soldiers shrieked it, then the rest took it up in a pandemonium of howling as

they turned in a mad, blind rush to escape from the room.

"No!" Adam yelled. "No, no, no!" and saw Lauder's face as panic-stricken as the rest being carried past him in the rush of bodies to the door.

He made a grab, caught Lauder, and was thrust away. His waving hands encountered the edge of the alchemist's desk as he fell backwards, and one of them closed over a brass paper-weight. He hauled himself up, swinging overhand with the weight as he came, and hurled it at the maniac yelling his triumph beside the crumbling beast-face in the flames.

The swing pulled him forward over the desk, breath sobbing in his throat, face crashing painfully into an ink-stand. He became aware of silence, with only the sound of his own breath in it, and pushed himself upright again. The warlock was lying spread-eagled in front of the furnace, blood trickling from the broken skin on one temple. The window and the door were jammed with soldiers turned to look at the still figure, and Lauder was approaching with a tight, nervous grin on his face. The room was filled with the stench of burning leather, and there was nothing to be seen in the furnace but a mass of black smouldering at the heart of the flame.

"It—it was only a trick, eh?" Lauder nodded to the charred mass in the furnace.

Adam shook his head. "Not even that! It was only a lucky chance for him that he happened to be burning the devil-disguise at the moment we burst in on him."

Tenderly he felt his injured face and added, "I thought Master Grahame had disposed of it before he fled, or I could have warned you of the warlock using it in some such way to scare you."

"And you are sure this is the warlock, not his alchemist twin?"

Lauder moved to stir the recumbent figure with his toe and Adam went to stand beside him.

"I am sure. But bring him round, and you will have the proof of it when he sees me."

Lauder dropped to one knee, but the warlock's eyes opened before he could reach out a hand to him. Their gaze rested briefly on Lauder's face, then travelled to that of Adam.

"Well, sir warlock," Adam challenged. "You see this is the

road to North Berwick all over again, but your brother is not here to save you this time. I wanted you killed then, although he did not, and now I will see to it myself."

He glanced swiftly, frowningly at Lauder, and told him, "I will borrow your sword if you please, Captain, and make a swift dispatch of this creature, although he deserves a more lingering death."

Lauder gaped at him. "Eh? Oh, my sword! Why, yes—" Grasping Adam's bluff at last, he made to unsheath his sword, but the warlock shot up a hand to stay the action.

"No, Captain! No!" he said breathlessly. "I am worth more alive than dead, can you not see? I am a witness—the most valuable witness the King could possibly have against Earl Bothwell. Take me to the King, Captain. *He* knows he cannot convict Bothwell without Richie Grahame!"

Lauder shook him off and rose to his feet. "I am answered," he told Adam grimly, "and the warlock shall have his wish."

"If you had known his brother—" Adam began, then stopped to glare down at the warlock, ashamed that he had ever mistaken him for his own Master Grahame. The height and the build were the same, of course, and the faces were identical; but where the lines on Master Grahame's face had all been of kindness and a certain weary good-humour, the lines on *this* face showed nothing but cunning and cruelty.

Lauder was looking past him to the troopers at the door. "Bind this prisoner's arms," he called, and some of the men came sheepishly forward to heave the warlock to his feet. Lauder steered Adam through the remainder until they stood together on the path outside the door. Adam nodded in the direction of Tranent.

"Back there," he remarked, "you said that Fian's confession would not be necessary now that we have his black book for evidence. Will the King still have him tortured, do you think?"

Lauder shrugged. "'Tis the Privy Council that orders torture, not the King. And once they have set the wheels of law in motion, nothing can halt them. Fian must speak, or suffer the worst that can be done to him."

"I think he will," Adam said quietly. "You saw how tranced his eyes were when we broke in to his house—

almost as if he were under some kind of spell. It must be a strange and powerful hold the warlock has over him."

He stood looking through the trees, thinking of the strange little man who was Dr. Fian, and added, "You remember I told you he was the only one of the witches who knew the secret of that mountebank in there. Yet somehow he has still managed to retain his belief that he is the Devil. Is that not a wonder?"

"I can tell you a greater wonder," Lauder remarked cheerfully. "This time to-morrow, your little witch will be free!"

"Aye," Adam agreed, "and you will have your promotion for capturing the warlock!"

"I daresay," Lauder answered smugly. "And so I will do something in return for you, young Adam, since I will owe that promotion to you. I will seek early audience of the King for the warrant to have Gilly released from the Tolbooth by noon to-morrow."

"Thanks, Lauder," Adam answered—awkwardly, because of the curious rush of emotion that was beginning to assail him as the full realisation of his achievement sank home; and they walked in companionable silence back to where their horses waited.

The troopers detailed to escort Fian were already there with their prisoner, and on a sudden impulse Adam went up to them.

"Speak up, for God's sake, sir," he urged Fian quietly, "or they will torture you again."

"Do not appeal to your God for me." Fian's reply came cold and measured out of the darkness. "I have my own god, and am faithfully sworn to him."

He was like Agnes Sampson, Adam thought helplessly; like Richie Grahame, like Bothwell glaring with those tawny flecks in his eyes—there was an evil sort of madness in all of them. The world would be well rid of such creatures! He walked away from Fian, and Lauder came up to whisper to him,

"We will take Richie Grahame to Mr. Justice Hart's house when we reach Edinburgh, and see him kept strait there. He must be held separate from Fian."

Raising his voice then he called out to Fian's escort, "Ride ahead with your prisoner, men, and mount a strict guard over him in the Tolbooth until my further orders."

Fian's escort moved off along the road to Edinburgh, and Lauder looked down the pathway between the trees to where his other troopers were marching Richard Grahame towards them.

"And you and I, Adam," he added, "will take the Devil to receive what is justly due him!"

"Amen," Adam responded soberly, and mounted his horse wondering how Gilly would take the news of her freedom.

Chapter 13

PRISONER'S RELEASE

She looked dazzled by the daylight when she stepped from the great door of the Tolbooth on the stroke of noon the next day. She shielded her eyes for a moment from the morning sun, glancing up the High Street, then saw him waiting for her in the portico of Saint Giles church opposite the prison door and moved towards him. Quietly she spoke his name.

"Adam."

"Gilly," he answered, as quietly.

"The alchemist?" she asked.

"Safe," he told her.

They stood staring at one another for a further moment, then for no reason that either could think of, they both suddenly burst out laughing.

"We can go home now," he told her, still laughing, and took her arm to guide her through the crowds of the busy High Street, but she pulled free again and faced him.

"Oh no, Adam, I am not going back to Master Seton's house. That is part of the past, and I am not going back to the past.

"These too!" She held out her wrists to show the red marks of prison fetters above her bandaged hands. "These are part of my past, and now that I have finished with them I want a new life."

"Wait," Adam told her carefully. "Let me understand you. Do you mean you are going to run away from Master Seton?"

Gilly nodded.

"And you are not afraid?"

"I have nothing to fear now except fear itself." Gilly smiled at him. "Breaking with the witches taught me that, Adam."

"But if you run away from Seton," Adam persisted, "you will be a thief. He owns your labour, and if you take that labour from him the law calls it stealing."

"Then I must bow to the law and be a thief," Gilly announced, "for I shall not go back to him. And so we had better part again now, Adam, unless—" She stopped to smile a challenge at him. "—unless you want to come with me?"

"Run away with you?" Adam stared at her.

"Why not? There is nothing to stop you, and we could manage very well together. You have some book learning, and I have a knowledge of herbs and cures that few can rival. We could drive a thriving trade between our talents."

Something had happened to Gilly in prison, Adam thought dazedly. Or was it simply that this was the true Gilly he was seeing—might have seen all along if her fear of the witches had not made something different of her? Certainly, she *looked* no less gentle, but she was still very far from being the timid, cowering creature he had expected to meet—in his secret heart had resigned himself to the burden of protecting again.

This Gilly could very well look after herself—not that she would need to do so, of course, if he did run away with her. He was perfectly capable of looking after them both. But she would certainly be no drag on him if he did—

"But I told you!" He interrupted his own thoughts aloud, reminding himself now as much as her. "If we run away we are thieves of our own labour, and the law will pursue us."

"Then we must go where the law will *not* pursue us," Gilly retorted. "We must go to England, where the law of Scotland does not apply—or so I learned in prison, and they are never wrong about such matters there."

"But where in England?" Adam asked, and without realising it began to move away as he spoke.

"To Berwick first, I think," Gilly said, moving with him. "That is just over the border, and not too far away. Then south to London, perhaps."

They were out of the shadow of the prison walls now, into the bright sunshine of the High Street, and the current of its busy life caught them. Adam quickened his step, enjoying the feel of the sun on his face and the ease with which his broad shoulders could forge a way through the crowd. Gilly stuck close to him, skipping every now and then to keep step with his longer stride and chattering on about this far-away place called London.

Her stories about it were only prison-gossip of course, Adam reminded himself, but it seemed a wonderful place all the same, and maybe there was good farming land round about it. He would have to find out about that!

He glanced down at Gilly's head bobbing beside him and thought they must look an odd pair among all these respectable townspeople—the little felon with her cropped head still carefully covered up, the prison marks still plain on her wrists, and the brawny country lad without even a whole shirt to his back. But Gilly's bonny hair would soon grow again. The marks of the fetters would not last. And as for himself, he was rich in experience at least, and oddly happy somehow, now that he was released from his own imprisoning hardness of feeling.

He grinned at some remark Gilly had just made. She caught his grin and they both burst out laughing again. "Hurry then," he told her, and seized her arm to swing them both deftly to one side of a passing water-carrier. "We have a long way to go yet!"

Neither of them noticed Dick Lauder as they passed by the gate-house of Holyrood Palace, but Lauder noticed them and stepped from the doorway of the gate-house to stare after them. They had been looking extraordinarily cheerful, he thought, and they were almost dancing their way along the path through the King's Park.

He watched them out of sight, chewing nervously at his lip as he speculated when he would get the promotion due him, and wondered suddenly if it was worth while when it seemed to have brought him none of the happiness these two had somehow found for themselves.

CATCH A KELPIE

If you enjoyed this book
you would probably enjoy our other Kelpies.

Here's a complete list to choose from:

for further details of Canongate Kelpies write to
Canongate Publishing, 17 Jeffrey Street, Edinburgh

A SOUND
OF TRUMPETS

In this exciting sequel to *Ribbon of Fire*, the
laird's tyrannical successors create unrest for
the islanders once more. Alasdair Stewart is
forbidden his promised education on the
mainland and is forced to work in another part
of the island. Here he learns of some new
treachery against his own people.

Tension builds as resistance to this news
mounts — burnt hayricks, a smashed beer-
cellar, the accidental death of one of the
landlord's men — all further excuses to bring
these rebellious islanders to heel. Lachlan Ban
promises to find a way to avoid meeting their
extortionate demands and a daring plot is
hatched.

In the hair-raising adventures that follow,
we see once again this master story-teller at his
fighting best. Is escape possible? Is exile
inevitable?

Allan
Campbell McLean

ROBBIE

Every morning Robbie hurtles down the
rough winding road to the school bus,
cheered on by his schoolfriends. Every
afternoon his grandfather meets him when
he comes home, and, as the the two explore
the Fife countryside the old man tells the
boy about 'the old times'.

In these stories Émil Pacholek vividly
describes Robbie's life as he grows up on a
farm in the 1950s. He tells of fun, adventures
and triumphs — and of Robbie's sadness.
The old traditions, like the village 'Harvest
Home', survive, but signs of the modern
world are all around and the Hawker
Hunters scream through the sky from the
military air station at Leuchars. Robbie's life
changes too, as he loses one companion
and cements his friendship with another.

Emil Pacholek

THE WELL AT THE WORLD'S END

Folk Tales of Scotland

This magical little book contains thrity-five folk and fairy tales, legends and some poems from almost every corner of Scotland, including Orkney and Shetlands, the West Highlands and the Lowlands. Some are taken from Gaelic translations, the richest area in Scottish folklore.

So intrigued were the authors by the stories they gathered, they decided to present them in English for easier reading for the wide audience they deserve rather than in dialect.

But it is the stories themselves, weird, comic and heroic, that make the book and invite us to live in a world where fairies, princes and monsters are a normal part of everyday life.

Norah and William Montgomerie

THE MAGIC WALKING STICK

Home from school for his half-term holiday, Bill acquires a walking-stick from a little wizened old man. He soon discovers that this stick has magic properties, capable of transporting him to any part of the world he wishes.

After some experiments and dangerous visits to such places as the Soloman Islands, the elephants' grave in Africa and a dramatic rescue trip in the Sahara desert, Bill discovers that there are two such magic sticks in the world. One is for gallivanting and amusement, the other for chivalrous deeds. Misuse of either stick would result in its disappearance.

Which one does Bill have?

No-one can tell an adventure story like John Buchan and in this tale his imagination and sense of excitement know no bounds as his hero performs daring deeds in the most unlikely places.

John Buchan